FREUD'S
Megalomania

FREUD'S
Megalomania

ISRAEL ROSENFIELD

W·W·NORTON & COMPANY
New York   London

For information or permission to reproduce selections
from this book, write to Permissions,
W. W. Norton & Company, Inc., 500 Fifth Avenue, New York, NY 10110

The text of this book is composed in Galliard
with the display set in Galliard
Composition by Tom Ernst
Manufacturing by Quebecor Printing, Fairfield Inc.
Book design by Jacques Chazaud

Library of Congress Cataloging-in-Publication Data
Rosenfield, Israel, 1939–
    Freud's Megalomania : a novel / Israel Rosenfield.
        p. cm.
    ISBN 0-393-04898-5
    1. Freud, Sigmund, 1856–1939—Fiction. 2. Psychoanalysts—
Austria—Fiction. I. Title.

PS3568.O8176 F73 2000
813'.54—dc21

                                                                00-020401

W. W. Norton & Company, Inc., 500 Fifth Avenue, New York, N.Y. 10110
www.wwnorton.com

W. W. Norton & Company Ltd., 10 Coptic Street, London WC1A 1PU

1 2 3 4 5 6 7 8 9 0

To Catherine

FREUD'S

Megalomania

With an Introduction and Notes by
Professor Albert J. Stewart

CONTENTS

Megalomania

INTRODUCTION

by PROFESSOR ALBERT J. STEWART

Every century has its ghosts. Some have exited gracefully, admitted their time was up and disappeared, leaving little trace of having been around. Others have been more troublesome. It was one of the remarkable features of the late twentieth century that when the advance of science and technology had made the idea of ghosts suspect, ghosts had, whether in revenge or because they too had benefited from the new technologies, created the greatest havoc known in history. And those who had sought to deny their existence had paid a price for their denials.

—Anonymous

I

I never liked Freud.

For a long time I believed he had been guilty of some of the worst intellectual brainwashing in history. I was more than pleased when the Academic Establishment had finally joined the chorus of indignant voices. If Freud has been thrown from the Olympian heights he once occupied, if he is no longer considered one of the great thinkers of history, if it is now known that he was a man who deceived, lied and cheated—a man who *invented* the psychiatric syndromes, the patients and the patients' stories to "prove" his theories—it should not be forgotten that the Age of Freudian Tyranny was in a not-so-distant past. Grammatical mistakes, mispronunciations, poor penmanship, broken legs, unattended stoves, marriage proposals and wallets absentmindedly left behind were scrutinized for incestuous and perverse desires; ordinary citizens were accused of crimes unbeknownst to them and their denials served as proof of guilt, just as denials of Freudian theoretical insights were proof of the truth of the theory.[1] What mattered was not what you knew about yourself, but what you didn't know. We were punished and ostracized for harboring demons deep inside our souls, demons we had never met and whose existence we had never suspected.

If Freud cannot be accused of creating war and devastation, still he caused untold suffering to countless individuals with his fraudulent therapies; he deluded them into believing they were controlled by nasty demons; he forced patients around the world to confess to desires and prurient interests that make the Marquis de Sade read like child's play. He created a profession that milked dry innocent people whose

[1] The Age of Freudian Tyranny has marred the careers of many. For details about a scholar who, in times of tyranny, was compelled to write Freudian analyses of literary works and came to see the error of his ways, see the Endnotes, p. 165.

"problems" a good spanking would have quickly cured; he convinced the weak-minded that they could recover and relive their past under the guidance of one of the trained members of his profession; he pretended to have uncovered the fundamental mechanisms of our habits, our desires, our loves, our hates and even our professional choices; he explained everything from the universal to the most intimate and private: History in the same breath as Greek Tragedy, a child's obsession with dolls, the shape of the Eiffel Tower, why women carry purses and why Gustav Mahler called his wife Alma, "Marie" and why *she* accepted to marry him in the first place.[2]

Nothing escaped the devastating revelations of Freudian theory or the scrutiny of his loyalists, unwavering in their belief and dedication to the Leader, the Teacher, the Master, the Man who had given

---

[2] Ernest Jones tells of the meeting between Mahler, who had become "distressed about his relationship to his wife," and Freud in Leiden in August 1908. "Although Mahler," Jones writes, "had had no previous contact with psychoanalysis, Freud said he had never met anyone who seemed to understand it so swiftly. Mahler was greatly impressed by a remark of Freud's: 'I take it that your mother was called Marie. I should surmise it from various hints in your conversation. How comes it that you married someone with another name, Alma, since your mother evidently played a dominating part in your life?' Mahler then told him that his wife's name was Alma Maria, but that he called her Marie! She was the daughter of a famous painter [*Mahler* in German]. . . so presumably a name played a part in her life also" (Ernest Jones, *The Life and Work of Sigmund Freud,* vol. 2, New York: Basic Books, 1955, p. 80).

meaning to their lives—as they would give meaning to the lives of future generations. Dissent was treated with a disdain that must have been the emotional equivalent of one millionth of a degree above absolute zero—the temperature at which atoms too behave identically.

Surely it is little wonder that most of us who were interested in studying the mind turned to what was new and unexplored—Cybernetics, Artificial Intelligence, Linguistics, Philosophy, Robotics and Neurophysiology—hoping to escape from the oppressive intellectual and scientific tyranny of the day. And perhaps to protect ourselves against the never-ending onslaught of psychoanalytic interpretation, we too had our gods and demigods, John von Neumann, Alan Turing, Kurt Gödel and Norbert Weiner. We were all very excited, for we were taking part in the birth of a new and powerful science. I and my colleagues were breaking new ground in our understanding of the mind, machines and the brain. We were one big family of happy "cogs."[3]

And then something happened that seems to have forever changed my view of what we had done and where we were going.

One day a woman of medium height with an uncommonly beautiful face came to my office. She introduced herself to me as Bernadette Schilder and

---

[3] "cog" = cognitive scientist

handed me a manuscript that she said was by Sigmund Freud.

The previous evening I had attended a rather raucous meeting of psychoanalysts, psychologists, philosophers and scientists.

As I've said, I've never liked Freud, but that evening I had had trouble swallowing the haughty "scientific" pretensions of Freud's most vocal critics. They mixed criticism of his methods and the untestability of his theories with questions about his personal ethics.[4] I was equally uncomfortable with the fanatical defenders of Freud and his theories. They spoke about the science of the mind as if it had started in 1899 and had stopped, with Freud's death, in 1939.

In my irritation I had said in public that though I didn't sympathize with Freud's defenders, they could have easily argued that the self-assured pretensions of his critics were misplaced. I had said that even if much has been learned about the brain in the last half century, we are still no closer to understanding the mys-

---

[4] Freud's relationship with his sister-in-law Minna has been the subject of considerable concern among Freud's detractors. Peter Gay, who has consistently defended Freud both as a man and a scientist, asked the Freud Archives if he could see the Freud–Minna correspondence between 1893 and 1910 and was told it was missing. Frederick Crews claims it can be found in Container Z3 (Frederick Crews, *The Memory Wars*, New York: A New York Review Book, 1995, p. 134). I am not sure what an affair between Minna and Freud would prove about Freudian theory or Freudian ethics.

teries of sex, desire, consciousness, walking, seeing, thinking, hypocrisy, deception and lying. And if "science," I explained, had discovered the importance of neurotransmitters in our states of depression, joy and anger, as interesting as that might be, knowing that there is more of a particular neurotransmitter when we are depressed does not explain depression any better than Freudian theory; nor does an analysis of neurotransmitter levels help us understand our feelings, why we have them, what causes them, how long they will last and how we can avoid them. I reminded the audience that we can't build robots in any way as threatening as Hollywood's celluloid clones of human intelligence.

My remarks were met with shouts from all sides of the auditorium and the meeting broke up before any semblance of order was restored. I received as many congratulations for my brief statement as I did warnings that my stupidity and blindness were sure to bring a quick and well-deserved end to my scientific career.

Bernadette Schilder, who tells her own story in the following pages, and the Freud *Manuscript* were, in a way, rewards for my boldness of the previous evening. I never would have predicted what I was about to learn, but even when I first met her there was something about this woman, something about the way she peeled off her coat and smiled, that told me she was going to break the routines.

But it was several weeks before I got around to

reading the *Manuscript*. After all, I certainly didn't expect anything of interest from a man who knew nothing about computers, the surface of the moon or DNA. As I have already said, I considered Freud no more relevant to late twentieth century science than Galen's theory of Humors and Aristotle's theory of motion.

When I finally did read it I had to marvel at the extraordinary power and relevance of the *Manuscript*. For not only does Freud recognize the inadequacies of his own work, but he raises questions about authority, power and knowledge that to my mind are new. Scholars, I am sure, will be taken aback by the fertility of Freud's mind in his final years. Even those most opposed to Freudian doctrines have not come up with criticisms as deep as those Freud has made in the *Manuscript*. Freud, more than any of his critics, foresaw not only the popular, scientific and scholarly reactions to his work in the half century after his death, but he understood the history of science with a depth that has been lacking even among philosophers of science. The ridicule to which Freud has been, and is being, subjected loses its force when we read the *Manuscript*.

Here Freud reveals a dark personal secret that he had succeeded in keeping from friends, family and the public eye for more than half a century.

Reexamining his own testimony at the trial of his friend from his student days, the Austrian Nobel Prize winner Julius Wagner-Jaurreg,[5] he comes to radical conclusions about the root causes of the widespread mental and physical breakdown of soldiers returning from duty at the front, conclusions that go well beyond the wartime experiences of these young men. The soldier at the front deludes himself about the reasons why he is there, as he does about his importance in battle; so too we are all forced into a state of almost constant self-deception because of the limits of our knowledge and understanding of our own and others' lives, as well as a deep misunderstanding about the nature of authority and our relation to it.

What is new and startling about the Freud of the *Manuscript* is the claim that human psychology would not be possible without self-deception, double-dealing, lying and reprisals. These are not idle faults of rational individuals; they are what being "rational" is all about. Neither the battle nor the promised rewards are in any way what they appear to be.

But it is certainly Freud's insight into the importance of emotions in a world of self-deception and lies

[5] Julius Wagner-Jaurreg (1857–1940; or Wagner von Jaurreg, often referred to as Wagner in the *Manuscript*) met Freud when the latter was a medical student in 1880. He received the Nobel Prize in Medicine or Physiology in 1928 for his Malaria-Fever Therapy that is discussed in the *Manuscript*. An opponent of psychoanalysis, Wagner maintained a friendly correspondence with Freud throughout his life. Wagner's trial in 1920 followed complaints from Austrian soldiers about certain practices in his clinic during the war. The story is discussed at length in Freud's *Manuscript*.

that is one of the master strokes of his essay. Since the limits of knowledge make it impossible for reason to tell us what to do, our emotions deceive us into believing in the "rightness" of our actions. What emerges from the *Manuscript* is an extraordinary grasp of the psychological roots of our survival in a world of the unpredictable.

While Freud had witnessed the beginnings of events that ultimately led to the collapse of political authority and ideologies, the *Manuscript* suggests that he may have begun to uncover, as well, the psychological roots of the extraordinary events, both political and scientific, that have so overwhelmed us these past decades. If anyone has come close to giving us a sense of how all that could have happened, I must say that the Freud of the *Manuscript* has.

There is much here to stimulate the neuroscientists as well. The genius of the contemporary biological sciences was, of course, unknown to Freud. Some of its more important ideas were inspired by the work of John von Neumann, and there is a striking relation between the theories of von Neumann and Freud.[6] This became known to me when I asked the Freud Archives if they knew anything about the *Manuscript*. At first they were puzzled.[7] But they eventually sent

---

[6] John von Neumann (1903–1957) was one of the leading mathematicians of the twentieth century. For more details, see Endnotes, pp. 165–166.

[7] See my Editorial Introduction, pp. 154–155.

me two papers and kindly gave me permission to print the papers with the *Manuscript*.

I will leave the pleasures of discovering the surprising contents of these papers to the reader. Personally I find Freud's record of his meetings with Gustave Eiffel's associate, Maurice Koechlin, among the most moving pieces of writing he left behind.[8] And as the reader will also discover for himself, it, and the Notes about von Neumann by Anna Freud, add to the richness of the original *Manuscript* and its relevance to today's science.

But there are deeper and more personal reasons for my finding the *Manuscript* so satisfying. That evening when Freud was being torn to shreds by the intellectual and scientific elite, one of the participants read to us a litany of the faults of Freud and the Freudians, a litany that was, as the reader will certainly agree, in no way foreign to my own thinking. What was read was the following:

The [Freudian] movement's anti-empirical features are legion. They include its cult of the founder's personality;

---

[8] Gustave Eiffel (1832–1925) is most famous for the three-hundred-dred meter tower that bears his name, built for the 1889 Universal Exposition in Paris. Maurice Koechlin (1856–1946) worked closely with Gustave Eiffel from 1879 to 1895. The relationship between the two men, in particular their respective roles in the building of the famous tower, is discussed in Freud's posthumous paper, "The Tower of Babel," which was found in the Archives, and which is printed here for the first time pp. 133–153.

its casually anecdotal approach to corroboration; its cavalier dismissal of its most besetting epistemic problem, that of suggestion; its habitual confusion of speculation with fact; its penchant for generalizing from a small number of imperfectly examined instances; its proliferation of theoretical entities bearing no testable referents; its lack of vigilance against self-contradiction; its selective reporting of data to fit the latest theoretical enthusiasm; . . . its indifference to rival claims and to mainstream science; . . . its insistence that only the initiated are entitled to criticize; its stigmatizing of disagreement as "resistance," along with the corollary that, as Freud put it, all such resistance constitutes "actual evidence in favour of the correctness" of the theory (SE 13:180)[9] and its narcissistic faith that, again in Freud's words, "applications of analysis are always confirmations of it as well" (SE 22:146) [Frederick Crews, *The Memory Wars*, New York: A New York Review Book, 1995, Note 24, pp. 61–62].

I agreed with all that. But what made me uncomfortable was that while this was true of Freud and the Freudians, it was also true of many of my colleagues as well.

None of this was very clearly articulated when I and my closest collaborator left on a lecture tour of Europe a few weeks after Bernadette Schilder's visit to my

[9] SE refers to *The Standard Edition of the Complete Psychological Works of Sigmund Freud,* general editor James Strachey, London: The Hogarth Press (volume and page numbers are given after "SE").

office. The tour ended in London and I had decided to take a brief vacation in Paris and then return to New York. Before I left, Norman had insisted on seeing me.

II

I first began reading the posthumous Freud manuscript on the Eurostar, somewhere in the tunnel between London and Paris. My state of mind at the time might best explain why I was—and remain—so impressed by this work.

It was ten minutes before five and Dicke—Norman Dicke, with whom I had coauthored more than forty scientific papers during our five-year collaboration—was standing in the entrance to Waterloo Station, clutching a FedEx package to his chest. Upon seeing me, he plunged his hand into the white envelope, removed a little blue book and thrust it under my nose as he opened it to the Acknowledgments. Pointing with his chubby index finger to the middle of the page, he said, "Read that!" and when I hesitated, repeated, "Read it!"

And so I read: "Albert Stewart was a critical and imaginative sounding board."

I closed the book, handed it back and walked into Waterloo Station.

I never would have thought that leaving a Looker Laureate standing in the middle of the street, a scowl on his face, his lower jaw hanging down, fists clenched as if he were about to deliver a right jab to my chin . . . no, I never would have thought that leaving him standing there just outside Waterloo Station would have given me so much pleasure. Norman Dicke, Looker Laureate, had been my closest colleague for more than five years. I used to look forward to seeing him—even hearing from him when inspiration suddenly struck at two, three or four in the morning. I had dined out on him, when I wasn't dining with him. He had so insinuated himself into my life that I'm not sure I wasn't walking around thinking of myself as Norman Dicke, the way biographers become the characters they're writing about.

Yes, I had left him standing there with his new book hot off the press and the FedEx wrapping still in his hand.

They had already made the last call for passengers for the five-forty, so I had to make my way through customs as quickly as possible. A deep feeling of regret welled up in me as I walked down the platform to car 23.

And yet I'm not sure what I regretted. I say I had dined out on Dicke. I had dined out on his quirks, his sudden changes of mood, his constant need for reassurance, his blanket dismissals of other scientists and *their* theories, his claims to professional talent in the arts—in music, literature and painting—and his need to hold court, as if there were no other person worthy of notice. He had had a disastrous relationship with his wife for more then twenty years, and occasional affairs that he felt compelled to give vague hints of to his postdocs. There were rumors of screen actresses, princesses and wives of other Laureates seduced and abandoned. I don't know if any of it was true.

But what Dicke was really all about (and the reader of the posthumous Freud manuscript is about to discover *why*) was *The* Theory, *Doctor* Norman Dicke's *Loop Theory*—conceived on the night of December 23rd, 1994, when a violent snowstorm grounded Dicke's one-engine plane in the Siberian town of Krasnoyarsk, where he had gone to help the Russians build their first robot for outer space. Unable to sleep, he had feverishly set down the equations of Loop Theory (the basis of the expanded version in the little blue book for which I had been the "sounding board" three years later)—a theory, I believed, that was at the heart of today's understanding of the human mind. My lectures around the world included slides of the tattered papers that Dicke brought back from Siberia, preserved to this day in the Institute vault. I was proud of these scribbled notes, as I was proud to be a colleague and intimate friend of Dicke's, because Loop Theory was the ultimate theory, the theory that would have left Plato, Pascal, Descartes, Leibniz, Boole, Turing, von Neumann and Einstein in awe. Loops describe the intricate and subtle ways the brain communicates with itself, with other brains, with our surroundings and ultimately with the universe as a whole. "We are loops and we loop." The profundity of the theory is matched only by its difficulty and obscu-rity; even if you grasped it, your understanding of its totality would last but for an instant. "You get it and it disappears," Dicke said.[10]

---

[10] There has been considerable confusion about the relation between Dicke's work and the widely popularized "Brain Paste Theory." The following exchange between Dicke and an unusually hostile journalist, I. D. Rappaport of *The Economist*, illustrates the misunderstanding (all the comments are, of course, Rappaport's, as printed in his article):

"That's just like Brain Paste, now, isn't it?" *The Economist* asked.

"Brain Paste?" Dicke repeated. He had turned white as a sheet. For what must have seemed like an eternity he sat there, all the features of his face completely frozen, staring at your reporter. "You're calling my Loops Brain Paste? Did I hear you right?" His tone of voice suggested criminal offense.

"Well, sure. There's a lot of talk around that Brain Paste Theory and Loop Theory are really different ways of saying the same thing. Some scientists say Loops is just an obscure way of talking about Paste. They say that Brain Paste Theory—that all brains have Paste, that Paste pastes, and that no two brains are pasted up the same way—is much clearer than talking about Loops and that Brain Paste has been found, whereas nobody has ever seen a Loop. Do you have any comment on that?"

"Do I have any comment on that? Yes, I have plenty of comment on that. You're no scientist and you just listen to me. I run the most prestigious brain laboratory in the world. Just you get that straight. There is no such thing as Brain Paste. Do you hear me? It's an experimental artifact. Brain Paste is just Loop Theory in drippy clothes. There's no paste there. If there were, it would be like a machine all gummed up. You couldn't think. Where's the thought in paste? Did you ever ask yourself that question? Go ask it of your scientists. Talking about being obscure. If Loops were paste, then

The most spectacular consequence of the theory and, to date, certainly one of the greatest scientific achievements of our day was the "Marilyn Machine."

Loops couldn't loop. It's the Loops that form a kind of Scotch tape, linking—that's the important word—linking and looping, you get it. When I wrote my 'Outline of the Theory of the Loop and the Mind,' I spoke about a mathematical paste—it's really too difficult to explain, there's just no good mathematics around to describe it, but that's what it is, mathematical paste, a mathematical paste that glues, mathematically speaking, of course, the brain together. That's where they got the idea of a paste. The rest of the article was too difficult for them to understand. Mathematics is what Loops are all about. You can't manufacture mathematical glue. It's like calling the plus sign of addition a glue. Addition isn't *pasting* numbers together. Adding uses a mathematical glue. The brain's got a mathematical glue too—in the Loops. But it's a lot more complicated than 'gluing' numbers together. It glues ideas, thoughts, you name it. Mathematically glues. That's what comes of trying to simplify mathematical and scientific ideas. It gets to be a gooey mess—a lot of glue! Brain Paste glue is like putting shit between papers and hoping they'll stick together. Sure they'll stick, but who wants the papers after that? That's what Brain Paste does to patients. Puts shit in their brains."

Nonetheless, the idea that our brains may be little more than glue might receive support from those who see all biology as reducible to physics. In an article entitled "And You're Glue," the physicist Frank Wilczek wrote: "It's a widely believed half-truth that protons and neutrons are made out of quarks. Actually physicists are increasingly discovering that it's considerably less than half the truth. . . . [T]he colour gluons, were once conceived as mere paste. . . .No longer. On closer inspection, the quarks appear as showier, but gluons as the weightier and more dynamic, constituents of matter." Also, "The closer we look, the more a proton (or neutron) appears as a bundle of soft glue" (*Nature*, vol. 400, 1 July 1999, 21–23).

As the Eurostar sped under three miles of earth and water, I couldn't help recalling the extraordinary performance of "Marilyn" in the Palazzo Vecchio in Florence the week before we had arrived in London; to the surprise of everyone—including Dicke—she had suddenly said, "*Mi piace*" (though the rest of her speech was incomprehensible). Then, two nights later, she again had made a special effort for her audience at the Royal Academy of Science with her "*Hôni soit qui . . .*" before trailing off into a noisy babble that didn't in any way diminish the audience's enthusiasm for our wondrous electronic creation.

Astonishingly, not only had Marilyn spoken appropriately in unfamiliar surroundings, Marilyn had also flirted with the public and had been proud of her "looks" and "body"—something that had puzzled even Dicke, since it wasn't clear to us just what Marilyn meant by her "looks," or what could have represented her body. Yet is was undeniable that this concern with looks and body proved how many of the real Marilyn Monroe's *thoughts* we had successfully captured in our machine. For if beauty is in the mind of the beholder, a machine that thinks of herself as having "looks" must have a mind. Marilyn was a triumph of Loop Theory.

Indeed, I had often heard it said that Dicke could only have sex when Marilyn was watching. Some women objected to her presence and he had to put her in the closet, but experienced women tended to be more tolerant. No woman I met—and I think that I had known them all during my years in Dicke's lab—could say what turned him on: her squeaky "Oh, darling," her imitation dance of the Seven Veils or just the idea that she was there watching him with another woman. After all, Marilyn was just a machine with an artificial sexy voice and a collection of erotic images.

But Dicke related to Marilyn as if she were a flesh-and-blood woman watching him have sex. He extolled her qualities to the half-naked women lying on the convertible bed along the wall of his office; he told them she was unique. There was no doubt that he became very excited in her presence.

But we all know—women, men and even the mice in the lab—that Dicke's greatest pleasure was to study himself. That was why Dicke spent so much time looking at himself in the mirror that he kept in the drawer of his desk. And that was why too Dicke carefully rehearsed every encounter—sexual, intellectual and casual—in his magical mirror. For it was only by careful rehearsal that Dicke could avoid the occasional grimace, the look of pain, that he so often *felt* but could not manifest in the presence of those who would call themselves his peers, his equals or simply fellow members of the human family. Dicke had no equals, a fact that he had to keep to himself in his normal intercourse with humanity.[11]

---

[11] In the *Manuscript* Wagner-Jaurreg (see Footnote 5 above) is discussed at considerable length. Freud's Wagner bears an uncan-

I had promised Bernadette Schilder and her editor that I would read and comment on the manuscript that I had been lugging around Europe; but, as the reader will understand, the trip was too exciting. A manuscript by Sigmund Freud couldn't compete with the success of Loop Theory (to which I had made important contributions of my own) and our Marilyn Machine. Freud would have had trouble grasping the elementary scientific truths that had made Marilyn possible, truths such as the widely accepted view that beliefs and desires are *physical* symbols in our brains— the atoms and molecules of our thoughts and emotions—and that these symbols collide with each other, change and give rise to new symbols . . . just as atoms collide and give rise to new atoms and molecules. Nor would he have understood that these truths permit us to understand *why* we have certain beliefs and desires, and *how* they change.

Questions about what makes us masochists or sadists, hysterics, obsessives, depressives or euphorics, what makes us brilliant or stupid, lovable or detestable, and what makes us law-abiding citizens, criminals, artists or scientists—questions that fill the columns of newspapers, that television pundits and journalists offer easy answers to—all these questions can now be

---

ny resemblance to Dicke. Of course, my understanding of Dicke may have been influenced by my reading of the Freud *Manuscript*, but I have good reasons to doubt that this is the case.

answered *scientifically*. The *physical* form of the *symbol* for masochism (or sadism, depression, joy, pleasure, etc.) in the brain is the *cause* of the *physical* act of masochism! It took the invention of the computer for such truths to be discovered, but today they would be obvious to any computer-literate four-year-old.

And where does that leave Freudian theory? Freud, with all his talk about symbols, failed to understand that it's not the *idea* that the symbol represents that makes us think and act as we do, but the *shape*, the *form* of the symbol that *causes* thought and action.[12]

But these pleasant thoughts of Marilyn and Loop Theory (and the irrelevance of Freudian theory) were suddenly wiped from my mind as the Eurostar plunged into the Channel tunnel. I was struck by the inevitable consequences of my behavior at Waterloo. When I had

---

[12] It is commonplace today for leading scientists and intellectuals to emphasize these fundamental, self-evident truths. Here are two widely read examples:

1. "If the bits of matter that constitute a symbol are arranged to bump into the bits of matter constituting another symbol in the right way, the symbols corresponding to one belief can give rise to new symbols corresponding to another belief logically related to it, which can give rise to other symbols corresponding to other beliefs, and so on" (Pinker, *How the Mind Works*, New York: W. W. Norton, 1997, p. 25).

2. "The physical properties onto which the structure of the symbols is mapped *are the very properties that cause the system to behave as it does*. In other words, the physical counterparts of the symbols, and their structural properties, *cause* the system's behavior" (Fodor & Pylyshyn in Haugeland, *Mind Design II*, Cambridge: MIT Press, 1997).

turned my back on Dicke, I had turned my back on the
intellectual and scientific excitement of those years of
collaboration. Never again would I find myself in the
eye of the hurricane, in the dizzying whirlwind of rapid-
ly advancing scientific discoveries that played havoc with
the old and paved the way for new and greater imaginative adventures. My collaboration with Norman Dicke
was over. Like his women, I had been seduced; and like
his women, at the least resistance to his tyrannical
needs, I would now be tossed into Dicke's bottomless
pit of oblivion. I had seen it before.

"Didn't you once collaborate with Albert Stewart?"
a naive journalist would ask one day.

"Never heard of him."

"But in your book you—"

"That was a misprint. Here's the corrected edition."[13]

---

[13] I don't know why (maybe a Freudian would have an explanation), but one of the postdocs, Debra, stuck in my mind that night
as the train plunged into the tunnel. What came to me was the
night we were dining at Il Mondo—it was Dicke's favorite, with a
lot of gondolas painted on the walls—and he was saying how in his
lecture earlier that day he had "blown the minds" of a group of
students with his usual talk about Marilyn. Nothing we hadn't
heard before. And then out of the blue Debra just blurted out,
"You should build a machine that makes pee-pee in its pants and
complains about the smell and dampness. That'll pack them in."
Dicke bit his tongue. I thought he'd say something sarcastic about
her having spent a year to think that one up, but he just stared at
her. And she added her *coup de grâce:* "What animal hasn't had to
piss?" Dicke tried to cajole her. He tried very hard. He called her a
"female philosopher of cloacal consciousness," said she was funny
and explained that you didn't have to be a Freudian to know that

The train had been a full ten minutes in the tunnel and the mirrored windows reflected the images of the passengers, all of whom, I decided, appeared somewhat troubled by the length of the ride. I was trying to concentrate on Dicke and me, but even those upsetting thoughts could not overcome the fear that possessed me as I realized that it had been less than a month since the reopening of the tunnel. Almost one year ago the Great Fire had left holiday travel plans on both sides of the Channel in total disarray. (The train seemed to be shaking more than usual, though I hadn't taken it for over a year and I wasn't sure if I accurately recalled my earlier experience.) It wasn't the equipment that troubled me, but the personnel who had allowed a burning train to enter the tunnel and continue at maximum speed until it was a two-thousand-degree mass of molten metal halfway across the Channel, where it was finally forced to come to a halt. To dispel my fear of being buried alive in the tunnel, I reached into my briefcase and pulled out the first thing my unsteady hand came upon. It was the Freud *Manuscript* that I

---

all her talk about "urinating" was just a flirt. He took on the airs of the world's greatest living scientist and brought the Big Bertha of his intellect into action. "I'm talking about biology, the biology of the mind," he told her. Personally, I couldn't have imagined a more *biological* question than urinating.

Debra finished her postdoc in another lab, but I've always believed Dicke was hoping she'd come begging that he take her back.

She never did.

had promised Bernadette Schilder and her editor I would read before I returned to New York.

And thus it was that I read Freud's *Megalomania* manuscript.

As the train rolled into the Gare du Nord, I read the last page. In our obsessions with Loops and Marilyn Machines, I thought, we had all missed the larger question of *our* obsessions themselves. And yet, in a curious way, hadn't the contemporary sciences been concerned with the very issues that Freud had so penetratingly analyzed in his posthumous work? Game Theory, Tit for Tat strategies, Prisoner's Dilemmas and Selfish Genes (as their very names suggest) are all about the same problems as Freud's *Megalomania*, but never quite get to the point.[14] Readers will learn more about this in Anna Freud's recollections of her conversation with John von Neumann that the Freud Archives allowed me to print at the end of this volume. In that conversation von Neumann's reluctant admission to Anna Freud that Game Theory was a failure—and this before its revival in Tit for Tat strategies and Selfish Genes—is much like Freud's admission of the failure of his psychoanalytic theories in the *Megalomania* manuscript. Both von Neumann and Freud ultimately rejected views that had been at the

---

[14] For a more extensive discussion of contemporary theories see the Endnotes, pp. 166–167.

heart of their respective theories, namely, that what we call morality, or moral law, derives from *strategic decisions based on self-interest*. If von Neumann's poker player was an expert in the art of bluffing, so was the Freudian unconscious. Whatever today's detractors of Freud might believe, von Neumann had taken what Freud called the unconscious and stuffed it into a logic machine. He says as much in his conversation with Anna Freud and, as Anna says, Freud would not have had any objections. On the contrary, he would have been very pleased to have been associated with von Neumann. Or at any rate, the post-*Megalomania* Freud would have been pleased.

The 47 bus rolled down the Boulevard Sebastopol. I couldn't help laughing to myself. It would have been difficult for me to find a better antidote to Dicke (and to my fear of the consequences of my having snubbed him at Waterloo) than the *Manuscript*. In the end, Freud's detractors had been right about the pre-*Manuscript* Freud. Freud would have agreed with them about his theories. But what they had failed to see was that the theories they considered real science—theories about Selfish Genes, Tit for Tat and physical symbols being pushed around in logic machines—were (as John von Neumann told Anna Freud) just a fancy rewrite of Freud—an update in the language of the latest technology!

Of course, Freud could not have known that his criticism of his own work would apply equally well to a new and exciting science that grew out of discoveries and inventions—above all DNA and the computer—that were made after he had died. Loop Theory is no closer to the truth than Freudian theory—which is not to say either is worthless. But it does warn us that moral and intellectual authority is not necessarily supported by any universal truths. On the contrary, as Freud has so movingly shown us in his posthumous work, there's an enormous amount of bluff in our science, our moral pronouncements and our everyday psychology. We have to bluff to fill in the huge gaps in our knowledge of ourselves. All you have to do is watch an MIT robot in action, or read the *scientific* explanation of consciousness, walking, vision, desire, thinking, memory, hypocrisy, deception and lying, and you would know that if Freud hadn't written the *Megalomania* manuscript, someone else would have done it.

But then why did it take more than half a century for this work to be discovered, a work that even Anna Freud apparently knew nothing about? That story, told on the following pages, is as extraordinary as the manuscript itself.

POSTSCRIPT: I have not seen Norman Dicke again.

NOTE ON THE
MANUSCRIPT

The *Manuscript* was translated by Bernadette Schilder. It was written in Freud's large, bold handwriting on the reverse side of writing paper from the Hotel Brésil in Paris. There are 127 numbered pages.

Bernadette Schilder explains how she acquired the *Manuscript* in her Preface. The two papers found in the Freud Archives leave no doubt that it is authentic. They too are written on stationery from the Hotel Brésil. "The Tower of Babel" essay makes an explicit reference to Wagner-Jaurreg that cannot be understood without reading the *Manuscript*. Indeed, scholars at the Freud Archives were unable to make any sense of this essay before the *Manuscript* was shown to them. In fact, the themes of "The Tower of Babel" essay illustrate some of the principal ideas that preoccupied Freud when he was writing his last major work.

However, certainly most startling is Anna Freud's reference to the hotel stationery on which Freud wrote the *Manuscript* in her "Notes on a Conversation with John von Neumann," though she apparently knew nothing about what Freud was writing at the time. Again Anna Freud's paper was familiar to the Archives scholars, but only became meaningful when they saw the *Manuscript*. I have already commented on the extraordinary relevance of this paper to present scientific and philosophical discussions as well as its deep link to Freud's posthumous work, a work that was apparently unknown to Anna Freud.

As much as possible, and without overburdening the text with unnecessary details, I have added footnotes giving biographical information about the individuals mentioned in Freud's text. I have also noted a parallel between the story of Freud's rapist and a remarkably similar recent story of a rapist in France, a parallel that gives added weight to Freud's discussion.

Since the *Manuscript* is, in some sense, Freud's final comment on his life and work, I have tried to note some of the important changes in Freud's views. I have also attempted to clarify scientific details that might be relevant to a contemporary understanding of the significance of Freud's posthumous work.

A number of intellectuals, scholars and scientists were asked to comment on the *Manuscript* before it was published and I have included some of those comments in the Endnotes. I regret that limits of space prevent me from printing all of the responses, which were of an extremely high quality. Rather, I have tried to include those comments about issues likely to be most controversial.

I hope that many questions will be answered by these notes and ask for the reader's indulgence for any obvious oversights on my part.

In addition to the Freud Archives, I want to thank the family of Maurice Koechlin for showing me and allowing me to print the passages from Koechlin's *Journal* included in the footnotes to "The Tower of Babel."

Finally, I would be more than remiss if I did not acknowledge that, in the preparation of the *Manuscript* for publication, I have been guided by the wisdom and insight of Bernadette Schilder, without whom this story never would have been known. For reasons the reader will learn, Freud dedicated the original work to her mother. I would like to dedicate my own, infinitely more modest, contribution to her.

—ALBERT J. STEWART

PREFACE

by BERNADETTE SCHILDER

I am one of Sigmund Freud's grandchildren. I have never met the other members of the Freud family and surely I am unknown to all of them, and to the scholars and psychoanalysts who in recent years have not hesitated to speculate on Freud's private life. My mother, Emma, was the daughter of Adelaide Benesch, Freud's mistress of many years.[1] She too is unknown to the Freud family and to scholars and psychoanalysts. But she was very much a part of his life. Adelaide was sixteen when she first met Freud on the train from Vienna to Berlin in 1916 and she last saw him a year before he died.

When I was a child we lived in London, where my mother worked as a translator. About a year before Grandmother died she told me that we owned a man-

---

[1] There is absolutely no mention of any mistress of Sigmund Freud's in any official or unofficial biographies. The name Adelaide Benesch never appears in any known Freud correspondence and the relevant documents in the Berlin City Hall were destroyed during the bombings of Berlin at the end of the Second World War.

uscript by Sigmund Freud that would one day be very valuable. She had never spoken about Freud before. And then a few days later I remember I was reading *Gulliver's Travels*, and my grandmother showed me a dream that Freud had analyzed in his book on dreams and in which he had cleaned a toilet seat by urinating on it and compared his dream to Gulliver's extinguishing the great fire in Lilliput with a stream of urine. I was very embarrassed by what she read to me, but my grandmother didn't seem to care. I found his dream rather disgusting and I told my grandmother so. She had laughed at me, and then she had said that it was true, he was a rather disgusting man, but if it hadn't been for him I wouldn't be here. She said that one day I would understand these things better and she wanted me to know that he was my grandfather. I was shocked that a man who could urinate on toilet seats to "clean" them was my grandfather. I was ashamed.

None of Freud's intimates knew about my grandmother. And, of course, none of them knew about the birth of my mother, Emma Benesch-Schilder, née Emma Benesch, on June 19th, 1923.[2] My grandmother called her Freud's Es [*Id* in German], because it was

[2] My father, Stefan Schilder, died in an automobile accident a year after I was born and my mother took back her maiden name, sometimes calling herself Benesch-Schilder, sometimes Benesch. Fortunately, she was listed in the London Directory as "Benesch, Emma," or, as the reader will discover shortly, Probst never would have found her.

in that year that Freud had published his book *The Ego and the Id*. Mother was a "terrible accident," for Freud the "blackest day" in his life.[3] He had tried to force my grandmother (Adelaide) to marry one of his associates and she had refused, reassuring him that he had nothing to fear from her. But Freud couldn't tolerate insubordination from family, friends or mistresses and for a long time after Mother was born he took his revenge and he refused to see my grandmother.

Mother was five years old when Freud first saw her in Paris, where my grandmother was working in a German bookstore. They lived in the Hotel Brésil.[4]

[3] Ernest Jones tells us that 1923 was the most depressing year in Freud's mature life, attributing his depression to the loss of his four-year-old grandson earlier that year: "Freud was extremely fond of the boy whom he called the most intelligent child he had ever encountered. . . . He died of military tuberculosis, aged four and a half, on June 19. It was the only occasion in his life when Freud was known to shed tears. . . . In the following month he wrote saying he was suffering from the first depression in his life, and there is little doubt that this may be ascribed to that loss, coming so soon as it did after the first intimations of his own lethal affliction" (Ernest Jones, *op. cit.,* vol. 2, pp. 96–97).

Of course, we will never know the reasons for Freud's depression, but the date of June 19th was also important to Freud because of the birth of his daughter Emma. It is certainly possible, as Bernadette Schilder suggests, that his depression was "caused" (at least in part) by the birth of his illegitimate daughter. In the passage in Jones just cited, he writes that Freud said his grandson "had stood to him for all children and grandchildren." There may be letters in the Archives that will shed more light on this story.

[4] Most of the hotel records from this period have not survived. However, the name "Benesch" was found on an old piece of

Freud had stayed there during his studies in Paris a year before his marriage.

When Freud saw my mother, he was so overwhelmed by her beauty that he expressed regret that he hadn't come to Paris sooner. He insisted that Grandmother return to Vienna so that he could see his daughter more often. He told Grandmother that she and my mother were the only bright lights in his life. But Grandmother refused to leave Paris and Freud became angry and jealous, accusing her of having affairs with his "worthless" former students.

Grandmother said he had always been an extremely jealous, dictatorial man who had been so spoiled by his parents, his wife, his children and those "worthless" students that he had taken it for granted that what he wished for would be. She said he cried like a baby when he left Paris: "I don't know if he cried like that with all his mistresses—or if he had any other mistresses—but it was a performance that I witnessed every time we parted company. Before your mother was born I thought there was something genuine about those crying fits, but the day I told him I was carrying your mother there were no tears! When I failed to follow his orders he cursed the day he met me."

But there must have been something genuine

---

abandoned luggage in the hotel storeroom. The corners of three envelopes with canceled stamps from Vienna and the dates May 7, 1928; October 23, 1929; and June (??), 1936, were found inside one of the inner pockets of the suitcase.

about his feelings for my mother because after he saw her in Paris Freud arranged to visit with her and my grandmother in Switzerland every three or four months.

The last time Grandmother saw Freud was when he was passing through Paris in June of 1938. He had insisted on seeing her with my mother, who was then fifteen years old.

Mother had seen Freud in Switzerland the previous year, and when he entered the hotel room in Paris she had been struck by how old and frail he had become. He was carrying a package that he carefully placed on the table in the middle of the room.

Grandmother said that Mother was already a "young lady" and that Freud was struck speechless by her beauty when he came into their room, but Mother told me that she had never felt any great affection for Freud. She said that he was always trying to please her and that he had a way of looking at her that made her uncomfortable. She remembered that on that occasion he had said to her that she looked exactly like her mother when he had first met her on the train to Berlin. Mother was irritated by this sentimental display.

Freud told her that he had a gift for her and opened the package containing a pile of papers with his large handwriting; she was very disappointed, a disappointment that Freud noticed. And when he told her that in a few years she could publish the papers, and that she could tell the story of how he,

Sigmund Freud, had fathered her, she felt a deep sense of disgust with the old man.

Grandmother too had been angered by Freud's presumptuousness. She said that Freud had been surprised by their indifference to his "gift" and just before leaving had hesitated and even taken the package from the table, suggesting that maybe they didn't want it. But Grandmother told him to leave it, that you didn't bring gifts and then walk out with them, and Freud just left the package and told my mother that he regretted he wouldn't know her when she was a grown woman. And he had added, placing his hand on the package, to the dismay of my mother and grandmother, that "this will guarantee your future. I've dedicated it to you." When he was gone my grandmother sat there looking at the package and shaking her head.

Several weeks later Grandmother decided to return the manuscript to Freud in Vienna. It was just after the Anschluss.

A number of years ago my mother received a call from a young man by the name of Heinrich Probst, who told her that he had a manuscript that he believed might have been dedicated to her.[5] Apparently, when Grandmother had returned the manuscript to Vienna it

---

[5] Heinrich Probst lives in Jena. His uncle, Georg Probst, had been Wagner's student in 1933 and told the young Probst that Wagner had nothing but contempt for Freud. Georg Probst shared Wagner's views.

had been seized by the Gestapo. The officer in charge had been a student of Wagner-Jaurreg, a friend of Freud's who subsequently turned against him. The officer decided to keep the manuscript, but forgot about it until several years after the war. He was on his deathbed when he gave it to his nephew Probst, telling him that it was a work of Freud's that he had seized during the war.[6] It was still in the envelope in which Grandmother had returned it from Paris.

When his uncle died, Probst brought it to a well-known German publisher and without explaining the origin of the manuscript said that he believed it was a work of Sigmund Freud's. As he explained to the publisher, even the best Freud scholars could not have known about the manuscript. But the publisher was not convinced and he told Probst that he did not believe the manuscript was authentic. He said that the handwriting was clearly not Freud's, that the content had nothing to do with Freudian thought and that he saw no reason why it would be of interest even as an anonymous work.[7]

Probst considered approaching the Freud Archives when he discovered among his uncle's papers my

---

[6] Georg Probst told his nephew that the *Manuscript* was a piece of anti-German propaganda that he was convinced would destroy Freud's reputation.

[7] Probst said that the German publisher, whom he refused to name, feared a repetition of the Hitler Diary fiasco.

grandmother's letter to Freud that his uncle had apparently removed from the envelope:

Mein Lieber,

I am sure that you thought that once you were gone I would immediately devour your "gift," but I am returning it to you unread. I'm sorry if you are impatiently waiting for a letter from me, or perhaps you expect a telegram, saying that I was so overwhelmed by the contents of what I assume may be your final work, that I had to contact you in haste and let you know not only how much I admire you but how much, in spite of everything, I love and adore you.

I haven't peeked inside. I don't know how you might explain that, but don't try to convince yourself that I read the manuscript and refuse to tell you because I am so overwhelmed by its contents. I know you are perfectly capable of believing that. Indeed, you will have the greatest difficulty—unless you have changed so radically in your old age—accepting the idea that I am just returning this to you unread.

I know you and I am sure that you have already begun to reassure yourself that it is only my infinite jealousy, my deep love of you etc. etc. that has led me to carry out this little charade. Funny thing, but I don't even care if you want to believe one of your own concoctions.

You said that this was a "gift" for my daughter. Well, so let it be. You should publish it now, so there

can be no doubt that you wrote it and no doubt that
she is your daughter. Or are you too cowardly, you
the man of international fame and prestige, are
you too cowardly to own up to your own actions as
you would help others own up to theirs?
Ihre Adelaide

I am sure that Grandmother never knew that Freud
didn't get her letter. She must have died thinking she
had called Freud's last bluff. And perhaps that would
have been the case if Freud had received the letter. But
we know he died never knowing that Grandmother
had returned the manuscript to him.

Armed with this new evidence, Probst went to several internationally known experts on Freud with his
manuscript. All agreed that the manuscript was not
written by Freud and that it would be scandalous to
allow its publication. He asked the experts if they had
any idea why the manuscript—even if it was a
forgery—would have been dedicated to someone
whose name—my mother's—was unknown to Freud
scholars and he was informed that it was the forger's
way of giving his or her own signature.

It was then that Probst decided to find my mother.
She and my grandmother had moved to London just
before the war. Probst came to us with the manuscript about a year and a half before Grandmother
died. After Grandmother died, Mother refused to
publish the manuscript.

I suppose my mother finally read it after the publication of one of those books about Freud's private life. My grandmother never said much about her feelings for Freud, but I know that my mother, who had been too young to know him well, had never forgotten their last encounter and deeply resented him. She resented, too, much that was being written about him. She told me that she didn't care what I did with the manuscript. The story of Freud's work and life had become so distorted since his death that she doubted that the publication of this manuscript would change anything. She didn't really care if I never published the work. She told me to give it to a publisher only if I had something to gain from its publication. And she warned me that there were so many "experts" on Freud and his work (none of whom she thought had anything of interest to say) that I would certainly be told, as Probst had been told, that the manuscript was not authentic. And, of course, nobody would believe how I had acquired it. Freud had insisted that Grandmother return all his letters to her, so there is today no evidence that Grandmother had been Freud's mistress for so many years.

Probably he didn't want the manuscript to be published during my mother's lifetime, for I suspect he knew she would have difficulty convincing a publisher of its authenticity. It is such a profound revision, if revision is the right word, of Freud's thinking that I wonder if he hadn't wanted it published at a time when he felt that his works would have begun to wear thin in the public mind and that only a scandal and a completely new argument would revive interest in him. And he had probably hoped that the purveyor of this new "theory" would be a wished-for grandchild. Because the manuscript is more than a new theory; implicit in it is the story of Freud's long affair with my grandmother. Not once, of course, is it mentioned. But it is the work of a man whose name has dominated the century, and yet he is a man who, by his own admission, has succeeded in keeping a dark secret from the public eye. And in one sense this manuscript is Freud's way of congratulating himself. It is at once a personal history and what I believe to be a rather deep addition to the most important psychological work of the century. It is about our darker side and certainly a comment upon the darker side of the life of a famous man. Freud's final joke was his hope that the authenticity of this work—perhaps the most genuine piece of writing of his life—would be forever in doubt. As Gulliver pissed on the fires of Lilliput, Freud will be forever pissing on the petty feuds of future generations.

I tell this story with no hope that it will be accepted by experts, scholars or even the general reading public. I am not hoping to set the record straight on Freud. Like today's experts, I never knew Freud. If I am, as my grandmother said, here because of him, I am not particularly grateful to him. My mother was an accident that he would have preferred to have avoided; but that accident having happened, he, in his cunning way, decided to turn it to his own advantage. The manuscript is what he left my mother and grandmother to remember him by; they gave it to me, knowing that the great man's "generosity" was a calculated gesture, in the hope that I might be able to benefit from it. Like the incest rules that seem to govern tribal behavior that so preoccupied my grandfather, I have always wanted to flee Freud and his family, as I suspect have other descendants of his who apparently have a "legitimate" claim to his name.

Nonetheless, when I read Freud's manuscript I was fascinated by its contents, not so much because of what it told me about Freud, but because of what it told me about myself, my friends and my acquaintances. There is something of the old devil in me too. I don't know if it came to me in my genes, or if circumstances have forced this nature upon me.

After I had read the manuscript I decided to translate some of it and I sent it off to a reputable American publisher, explaining that this was an unknown work of Freud's that I had discovered in circumstances I would be prepared to detail if he was interested in publishing it. I enclosed a copy of a few pages of the original text, along with copies of several manuscript pages from some of Freud's better-known works, so that the publisher could note the similarity of the handwriting.

I had done the translation at idle moments and I did not feel particularly pressed to complete the work. I had misgivings I was bothering at all, but I had a nagging curiosity. I did want to know how the "experts" would react to the manuscript, without knowing the full story of how I had come to acquire it.

Within a month I received a letter informing me that the manuscript was a fraud, that the handwriting was "so much like the writing in Freud's known works, that it is clearly an imitation. Our handwriting experts have noted that nobody always writes in exactly the same way. This is too good an imitation to be authentic."

The "experts" had also determined that Freud "would never have expressed any of the ideas in the pages you have submitted to us. It's just not the Freud we know. And it is not possible that a man's ideas could change so radically. The question of megalomania was an issue that was of no interest to Freud and, our experts believe, for good reason. As one of our readers noted, 'Megalomania sheds absolutely no light on fundamental questions of human psychology.' "

With that I was prepared to lay my project to rest.

One day, quite by chance, under circumstances that I need not relate here, I discovered the name of one of the publisher's "experts"—indeed I suspect there had only been one. In time I would learn that he is a man who has Freud's ego, but not his intellect, a man whose overriding ambition is to win for himself an even greater reputation than that of Freud's. But I didn't know that at the time. And so I decided to translate the entire manuscript. I was prepared to seek the assistance of the more legitimate members of my family to see to its publication.

When I had finally submitted the completed translation to publishers, I found myself pleasantly surprised. I don't know if the "experts" have changed their minds, or if there is something in the air these days. I'm sure my grandmother would have said that my sudden change of fortune had been all a part of Freud's calculations. Maybe she would have been right.

But as I prepared the manuscript for publication, I was troubled: I didn't doubt its authenticity, though I sometimes wondered if the copy I had—a copy that my grandmother had never read—hadn't been doctored, altered or somehow tampered with by the Gestapo; neither was I worried about the reaction of Freudian scholars and psychoanalysts, who, I knew, would have great difficulty accepting a work that would inevitably cast serious doubt on their authority, the prospect of which I enjoyed as much as I imagined my grandfather would have enjoyed.

What troubled me was perhaps the irrelevancy of the argument, the thought that my mother, or even my grandmother, had missed the opportunity and that now it was too late. The days of Freud's glory were gone and there was no way an unknown manuscript could revive them. Science had moved on. What I was about to publish was a curiosity at best, and if it was a curiosity, so was I. The secret I had been harboring all these years would prove to be about a trivial work and my claims to the family name would be dismissed or ignored.

So Freud had had a mistress. Scholars had been saying that for a long time; and any attentive reader of Freud would have noticed the clues he himself had left behind. I had no proof of the authenticity of the manuscript other than the manuscript itself and I knew this could be attacked as a forgery.

And if it was trivial, if it was out of date, the question of authenticity was of no great concern. Maybe deep down this is the reason I have never wanted to talk about myself. I feared the ridicule of others and I feared discovering something that would prove that my whole life has been built on an illusion. I have always wished that there would be some proof that would put my own doubts to rest and I have wondered where such proof might be sought.[8]

[8] When I had first read this moving account, I was reminded of the discussion that evening when Freud's detractors had had so much to say about the deceitful Freud. Here was the real deceit that none of the discussants knew anything about. But it was somehow different; there had been something empty and meaningless about the discussion, as if the discussants had been looking for a scandal that would make their case. It was obvious that Bernadette would have had nothing to do with the scandalmongering of the previous evening. She was proud of her story, proud of her grandfather. Her resentments were private, like the resentments we all harbor and that have meaning for us and us alone. Deceit was not her concern.

Megalomania

—*To Emma Benesch (Freud),*[1]
7 January 1938

1. An Apparent Oversight

*N*ot very long ago I wrote that to deny a people the
man whom it praises as the greatest of its sons is
not a deed to be undertaken lightly—especially when one
belongs oneself to that people.[2] I had no sooner finished
writing that sentence than I found myself paralyzed and
unable to continue.

I had wanted to write a book about the origins of the
Jewish people and the deep-seated resentment toward
them throughout history. My plan had been to write a historical novel, though I am neither historian nor artist, for I
thought that this was the best way to answer the question
that had preoccupied me for so long, how one man could
effectively create a "people" from a collection of individu-

[1] Emma Benesch married Stefan Schilder in Blackpool,
England, in 1954. Stefan Schilder was killed crossing Fulham
Road in London on June 19th, 1956, one year after the birth of
Bernadette Schilder.

[2] This is the opening sentence of *Moses and Monotheism*.
Perhaps in repeating the opening sentence of the Moses book
Freud is revealing that his deep concern with the Moses myth
stems from a desire to debunk all heroes. See Footnote 1, p. 119,
for more details about Freud's concern with Moses.

als who cared little about each other and had no desire to form any permanent associations. What is more, Moses not only effectively united these disparate individuals and families, but stamped them with a character that they would retain for thousands of years.

When I had completed my book The Man Moses (Der Mann Moses) I realized that what had truly preoccupied me for the past quarter of a century was the psychology of the man, Moses, not the psychology of his followers. I had created a theory that, I believed, could answer the second question, but I had no idea about the first, ultimately far more important and revealing, question—the psychology of men who are accepted as authorities.

Psychoanalysis has taught us that such apparent oversights are certainly not accidental and, of course, what suddenly upset me when I recognized that I had been avoiding the very question that troubled me the most was that the foundations of my life's work, psychoanalysis, the very tool that now revealed to me the inadequacy of my own investigations, was crumbling before my very own eyes as my life was drawing to a close.

I had always known that the fate of all scientific endeavors is oblivion and that the lucky scientist dies well before the first cracks appear in his edifice. But having spent the greater part of life confronted by the scorn and ridicule of men whom I knew were my intellectual inferiors, it appeared to me to be a cruel fate to end my days knowing that history would praise my enemies and throw my books into the scrap heap of past stupidities.

For sure progress depends on the ability of future generations to dismiss the past. Airplanes were not developed because men sang the praises of Icarus flapping his waxen wings.

But then it would be a mistake to assume that the recognition of the inadequacy of one's own work means that work is absurd or meaningless. It is in our failings that we often recognize not only truths about ourselves, but the nature of social and cultural pressures that have, as I have discussed in my earlier book Civilization and Its Discontents, driven us to a despair out of which has emerged some of the greatest achievements of mankind.

I make no such claims of greatness for myself, but I admit that as my days are numbered and as I reread some of the works that I had once considered my most important contributions to our understanding of human psychology, there is a constant sense of expectation, a sense that I am about to come upon some insight that will astonish future readers as much as it might continue to astonish me. But as I read on I have the feeling that I have disappointed my reader, as I now confess I have disappointed myself; the sudden sense of understanding is just not there.

I have criticized religions for creating a false sense of security in the face of the unknown by forcibly imposing an infantile mentality and mass-delusion; and I have written that the depth of religious feeling is only fully understandable if we recognize its infantile source: the conviction of the irresistible, all-embracing power of a

god—the need for being given a set of laws that must be
obeyed—comes from the same admiration, awe and grati-
tude that the child, confronted by the lawless world, shows
to the law-giving father. I have not hesitated to see in religious explanations attempts at fulfilling childish fantasies.
And now, with a force that time makes all the more
unbearable, I see in my own work some of the very childish fantasies that I have so harshly criticized in religion.[3]

I have concerned myself with the details of the stories we
tell about ourselves and I have found in those stories the
deceptions and the distortions that, I have argued, hide
often contradictory and unacceptable desires that we are
only able to master and control with our extraordinary
capacity for self-deception. I have seen self-deception as a
universal trait of the species, but I have never asked myself
if self-deception does not have the status of a primary characteristic of human psychology, if it is not the bedrock on
which all else, including civilization, is founded.[4]

I created psychoanalysis, after all, to control, if not, I

---

[3] Freud clearly has in mind the Oedipus complex. His failure to
name it suggests a disgust with his own invention.

[4] Freud never used the term "self-deception" before writing
the *Manuscript*. Here he fails to say that this is a radically new
view of his own work. Perhaps he finds the new view so convincing and powerful that he wants to lull the reader into believing
that it was always in his mind. The reader should, however, be
aware that, as I have already mentioned in my Preface, self-deception was certainly implicit in much of Freud's work. This view is
further elaborated in Anna Freud's discussion with John von
Neumann, which is included at the end of this volume.

must confess, naively, to eliminate a lack of self-awareness. But now, as I look over the many discoveries of psychoanalysis, I see that the forces that cement together the psyche are of such a nature that we can never recognize within ourselves, we can never tolerate knowing, just how deeply miserable we all are; and therefore we cannot know just how these forces drive us to constantly deceive ourselves in our self-observations and in our observations of others.

It is the mechanisms of the psyche, not our needs and our desires confronted by unbearable familial and social pressures as I had once believed, that are at the root of this self-deception. Psychology exists because of these mechanisms; no matter how hard we try to correct them, to evade them or to outwit them, we will inevitably be the greater fool.[5] We have tried and self-deception has won out through greater and more subtle subterfuges.

The history of human psychology is the history of these subterfuges, whose subtlety and nastiness has only increased over time. The remarkable progress we have made in our understanding of the material world can only be matched in our understanding of ourselves, if the cement of self-deception that is so central to maintaining even a modicum of our psychological equilibrium can somehow be dissolved, torn asunder and rendered harmless. I don't know if we will ever have the power to do this; and if we do, we will have

[5] This is an entirely new idea in Freud. He had always said that psychology exists because of the Oedipal complex. And yet the Oedipal story is ultimately one of self-deception, as Freud appears to have concluded himself in the *Manuscript*.

to confront a psychology that has little to do with our present selves. Indeed, I fear that if we could destroy the cement of the psyche, we would destroy the psyche in all its essential characteristics. I am not sure that is either desirable or possible.

The problem is not that we cannot recognize that what we say about our thoughts and actions is, at best, incoherent; we can and do recognize this after the fact. But once having admitted to ourselves our own subterfuges we are confronted by newer forms, which again we only recognize after the fact. We can never at the moment itself be honest with ourselves, never really understand when we are acting out what we are truly all about. It is only in retrospect that we can explain ourselves, and this retrospective view is hardly reassuring because it does so little to alter our behavior in the future.

Indeed, it is not honesty about ourselves that we are seeking, but a vague recognition that if we cannot really control ourselves, if we can only in retrospect understand what we are all about (and then even our retrospective view is hardly reassuring, since it is inevitably distorted by oversights that we try to fill in to create a coherent view of ourselves), we can hardly claim to understand the motives and actions of those around us.

It is our failure to be reassured about others, our recognition that whatever explanations others might give us must also be distorted by the same mechanisms that seem so beyond our control—that is what is truly disturbing. Because if we are constantly deceiving ourselves concerning our own motives and actions, certainly those deceptions are ultimately turned to our own benefit. But we know that we are doing likewise with family, friends and acquaintances and that therefore they must be doing the same.

And we know that there is thus a limit to our understanding of our relations with others, and our ability to rely on others, that we cannot go beyond. The recognition of this fact is not clearly articulated, but felt, sensed, in a deep and disturbing way. It is what ultimately makes us wary, suspicious of each and every person we know, a suspicion that we learn to control either by ignoring it, and hence accepting the deceptions of the others—chalking them up to so much dishonesty on their part—or allowing our suspicions to become an overwhelming sense of distrust that can paralyze our lives.

Those who become paralyzed we see in our clinics and we label them paranoid. We comfort ourselves saying that some paranoia is justified, but theirs has gone beyond what is reasonable. But this is a strategy of survival for us.

Suspicion in a moderate form we consider tolerable and reasonable, because this is what is most reassuring for most of us. Yet this "normal" form of suspicion and what we want to call its pathological form—paranoia—are not the only forms in which self-deception can manifest itself.

Far more important is that the whole of society ultimately rests on our distrust of each other, our need for rules and regulations that are forcibly enforced; culture is the consequence of this distrust, these rules and organizations that we have created in order to reassure ourselves about the others.[6] And it is the psychic mechanisms behind this transformation of distrust into culture that only now I am beginning to perceive, having spent most of my life uncovering the little foibles and distortions that are part of our everyday thought and action.

Indeed, if we could not deceive others and ourselves we would have no imagination, no thoughts, no pleasures, no pains, no defense against others, no desires to know others—no society, and most important of all, no notion of being, no sense of self, such that no one can ever possess us or know us in our entirety. Self-deception is at the root of society, but it is so transformed—for if it were not, society even as we know it would not be possible—that we do not recognize it. Inevitably it breaks down and we have periods of social and political crisis, ultimately wars, the roots of which we do not understand, because their psychological causes have been so distorted.

---

[6] While Freud never wrote anything like this before, it is not unrelated to the following passage in *Civilization and Its Discontents*:

The commandment, "Love thy neighbour as thyself," is the strongest defense against human aggressiveness. . . . The commandment is impossible to fulfill; such an enormous inflation of love can only lower its value, . . . [A]nyone who follows such a precept in present-day civilization only puts himself at a disadvantage vis-à-vis the person who disregards it.

Law is self-deception's answer to paranoia. And behind law, behind the notion of law and our psychic ability to accept it—even though we all know it does not and cannot work (or why would we need to constantly rewrite our laws?)—is the paranoia that we all have and that we accept within ourselves, puzzled by it, even dismissing it, and rarely recognizing it for what it truly is, though certainly prepared to see it when necessary in others. We can have a clarity and insightfulness about our friends' and neighbors' states of self-deception that we can never accept about our-selves. Nor would we ever be so foolhardy as to insist on the blindness of others. We only hint at what we think and what we understand about those who are close to us; we are wise enough to keep silent about our greater insights, if real insights they are.

But if the psyche is capable of such subterfuge, it would be wrong to assume that our self-deceptions must limit themselves to a vague sense of distrust and, in the more pathological cases, paranoia. Law may ultimately be the product of paranoia, but no citizen, no lawmaker would ever describe legitimate law as the product of a paranoid mentali-ty. Law is paranoia transformed, disguised so that we can no longer recognize it for what it is.

(Indeed, law is but a symptom of a more general prob-lem—the enormous complexity of our relation to our-selves, others and our surroundings; our knowledge will always be too limited for us to understand why we have so acted in the past, or how we should act now or in the

future. *If we were* completely rational *we would never be able to ever decide what to do.*[7] *We would never* know *enough. Thus our emotions create the illusion in us of what we want or desire. In deceiving us our emotions make us act.)*[8]

Hence *if there was one lesson I learned from psychoanalysis, it was the lesson of self-deception. The more I tried to distance myself from my patients' constant diversions, the more I found myself trapped by them in unexpected ways.*

---

[7] This explains, at least in part, the paralysis of the soldiers Freud discusses on pp. 91–92.

[8] The idea that emotions are at the root of our self-deceptions is, perhaps, a broader view of Freud's claim that love is an "overevaluation" of the loved one. For example, in 1905 Freud wrote, "A combination of exclusive attachment and credulous obedience is in general among the characteristics of love" (*Psychical [or Mental] Treatment*, SE 7: 296).

In 1920 he wrote in *Group Psychology* (SE 18:112):

In connection with this question of being in love we have always been struck by the phenomenon of sexual overevaluation—the fact that the loved object enjoys a certain amount of freedom from criticism, and that all its characteristics are valued more highly than those of people who are not loved. If the sensual impulses are more or less effectively repressed or set aside, the illusion is produced that the object has come to be sensually loved on account of its spiritual merits, whereas on the contrary these merits may really only have been lent to it by its sensual charm.

These views are consistent with the well-known clinical observations in Frontal Lobe Syndromes with a severe emotional deprivation, in which patients appear to be rational but are incapable of making decisions.

But, as I will explain, I think I have come to understand why psychoanalysis was doomed. The reasons were deeper and other than I had supposed. For within the confines of analysis I was never able to advance any theoretical arguments about the nature of self-deception and paranoia. I had put the question aside because any new science cannot try to tackle too many questions at once, and we had begun to establish, I thought, a solid understanding of the nature of neuroses. If our treatments were not always as effective as we might have desired, there was, I believed, the problem of resistances that manifests itself in so many unpredictable ways that we could not be blamed for our inability to break them down.

But I always knew that I would, if time permitted, one day have to confront the deeper questions of our self-deceptions and ultimately the paranoid personality that I had for so long ignored in the interest of the advance of our young science.

As we gingerly construct new buildings, monuments that have never been seen before, we have to create a scaffolding that will eventually be thrown out. Future theorists will find it easy to point back at me and laugh at the crudeness of the structures I have had to produce, at the cords and pulleys I have installed in my scaffolding, the cranes I have used to haul up the building blocks of an edifice that is only barely visible though the scaffolding. Surely the cranes, the pulleys and the cords have nothing to do with the final structure; yet knowing we may never see the final edifice, we can often become enamored of the scaffolding itself (for it has its own beauty), and this can lead to a certain amount of confusion. How we construct our buildings and theories is instructive in itself. Our constructions are limited by engineering techniques, as our scientific theories are limited by our mathematical and logical skills; and it is only over time that subtle new structures, new understandings that had been hidden from view, will begin to take shape.

The recent recollection of a series of personal events that I had long since put out of my mind has made me aware that I have overlooked critical issues in the theory of psychoanalysis. Certainly, had I tried to overcome the weakness of the theory earlier on, I would have been confronted by insurmountable difficulties. However, leaving it in its present state, fully aware of the theory's limitations, would be both dishonest and misleading for the future.

The circumstances that awoke within me a recognition of my theoretical oversights concerned one of my oldest acquaintances from my years in medical school, a man who was to become the most honored member of the medical profession in Vienna during my lifetime, Julius Wagner-Jaurreg. Wagner's name came up in connection with a scandal that had become the preoccupation of Vienna, a story to which I will now turn.

2. The Rape

*O*n a hot summer afternoon in late August 1931, two young German women were sunning themselves on a beach near S—— A——. They had been staying in a farmhouse not far from the shore where they had been visiting an old uncle of one of the young women.[1] About six o'clock in the evening, as the sun was beginning to descend in the sky, the young women climbed a road leading from the sea to the interior.

Earlier the women had been amused by a young man who had been showing off on the beach, running along the edge of the water, doing somersaults and splashing in the water. The women had reached the high point of the road and had stopped to admire the panoramic view of the

---

[1] It is well-known that to protect the identity of his patients and to clarify what was often a complex clinical picture, Freud often used the stories of more than one patient in his clinical narratives, at times (it has been claimed) even inventing some details himself. While much of Freud's story in the *Manuscript* cannot be confirmed because of the disappearance of court records and newspaper archives during the war, Freud's narrative bears a remarkable resemblance to the case of Luc Tangorre in France that is detailed in the Endnotes on pp. 167–168.

coast. As they stood there they heard the sound of an approaching motorcar.

When the automobile suddenly appeared, they were surprised and a bit frightened as it approached and came to a complete halt beside them. They were relieved to see the young man whom they had been watching earlier on the beach at the wheel of the motorcar.

He had a generous, soft face that, they later said, revealed a slight hint of mockery. He opened the door of his motorcar and, standing on the running board, offered to drive the two young women home. The younger of the women was rather shy and shook her head without saying anything, but her companion was amused and flattered by the offer and said that it would be fun to drive through the countryside at that hour.

The young man said that he didn't want to insist and if her friend did not want to join them it was perhaps better that he continue on his way without them. But the older of the two women insisted and finally they stepped onto the running board and the younger woman seated herself in the back while her friend joined the young man in the front seat of the motorcar.

As the car started and rounded a sharp curve, a neatly tied package slid across the backseat, gently pressing into the ribs of the young woman. Startled, she looked at it and noticed that it contained about a dozen copies of what appeared to be the same book. She was about to ask the driver what was in the package when he turned around and became agitated as she ran her hand over it and attempted to look inside the wrapping. He slid the package back across the seat and gave her a momentary look of disapproval that frightened her.

It was then that she noticed they were no longer driving on the road the women usually took on their way home to the farm and she voiced her concern. But her friend, who was enjoying her little flirtation with the young man, said that she should admire the view rather than worry so much.

Then, as the motorcar turned into a small dirt road and they entered into a vineyard, the older woman too became concerned. Once again the package of books slid across the seat and as the younger woman nervously pushed the package away the wrapping tore and she recognized a photo of the driver on the cover of the book. Her eye had caught the word "Innocent" when the driver abruptly halted the car and turned to her and said, "You shouldn't have done that."

He pushed the books back across the seat, opened the door of the car and pulled the young woman out of the motorcar. She struggled with him for several minutes as her friend, who was watching in horror, sat paralyzed while the young man beat her, ripped her clothes and raped her. He then yanked the older woman from the front seat and beat and raped her too. He left the two women lying there and drove off as the sun began to set.

It was three months later, when another rape was

reported in the same region, that the young women went to the police. When the women told the story of the neatly wrapped pile of books, the police showed them a copy of a book entitled Innocent but Guilty[2] with a picture of the young man, Hans Hellbach, on the cover and the young women immediately identified their aggressor.

The police questioned them closely, suggesting that they were not dealing with the man whose picture was on the cover of the book, but an imitator. The young women insisted, and several weeks later a young man was arrested whom the women identified as the man who had raped them and who was indeed the subject of the dozen or so copies of the book that had been neatly wrapped and tied in the backseat of the motorcar. The author of the book was a Polish "neurologist," M. Kozlowski.[3]

In Austria the story of Hellbach became a cause célèbre. Hellbach had been arrested on a number of previous occasions for rape and each time had been released, until a series of rapes occurred in southern Germany in 1927. Following his arrest in 1927, he was convicted and sentenced to a long prison term. Hellbach continued to maintain his innocence and in 1929 a number of prominent

---

[2] In the case of the French rapist, a book entitled *Coupable à tout prix* [*Guilty at Any Price*] by a French researcher at the CNRS, G. Tichané, was published in 1984.

[3] Michael Kozlowski (1861–1935) was born in Poland, received his medical degree in Kraków in 1895 and fled to Vienna at the beginning of the First World War. He was a colleague and friend of Wagner-Jaurreg.

Austrians filed a petition with the government seeking
amnesty for him, among them the recent Nobel laureate
Wagner-Jaurreg.

Wagner had known Hellbach during the Great War,
when he had treated him in his famous clinic. Hellbach
had been wounded and, following his recovery from what
were described as "minor injuries," had developed a paralysis of the right arm. The authorities had accused him of
simulating his paralysis and had sent him to Wagner's clinic, where he was treated and "cured." He then returned to
the front, where he distinguished himself in several important engagements, and after the war Wagner often cited
him as an excellent example of the efficacy of his "cure."

In a curious way the Hellbach affair had awakened within me a deep sense of personal failure that is associated in
my mind with Wagner's "cure." For Hellbach was but one
example of many Austrian soldiers who had become paralyzed and had been treated by Wagner. If I had believed
that I had understood the limitations of Wagner's work
and I was prepared to accept that my own explanations
were, at best, inadequate, only now do I realize just how
shattered were the psyches of these young soldiers, and
how blind both Wagner and I were to the true nature of
their psychological and physical breakdown.

3. The Malingerers

*D*uring the first years of the Great War many
Austrian soldiers had suffered wounds of varying
severity and were treated in hospitals near the front, where
they subsequently developed symptoms that appeared to
be hysterical—severe trembling and paralyses of their arms
and legs. What were subsequently called the War Neuroses
became a veritable epidemic in the Austrian army and the
authorities feared that the war would be lost because the
ranks of the army were being depleted by a widespread
outbreak of hysterical symptoms.

Though I was not familiar with the problem at the time,
the diagnosis and treatment of neuroses was, of course, the
one area where the new science of psychoanalysis, which I
am personally responsible for the creation and development of, had made important contributions. But the
Austrian authorities were well aware of the generally hostile feelings of the medical profession to my work and
therefore never sought any advice from me. I cannot fault
the Austrian leadership, as we were in the middle of a terrible war and the pressures of time were too great for the

government to become embroiled in any controversy. It made perfect sense for the authorities to turn to Vienna's best-known psychologist, Julius Wagner-Jaurreg.

Wagner created a clinic for the "treatment" of our soldiers. I am certain that his motives were wholly patriotic and I cannot blame him if his unflattering view of psychoanalysis prevented him from seeing the pitfalls into which the government was dragging him. It was his firm, and I believe honest, conviction that our soldiers could be quickly and effectively treated with new electric therapies that were becoming popular in psychological clinics throughout Germany at the time. He found a particularly sympathetic colleague in Kozlowski and in the early years of the war Wagner's clinic became an essential part of the war effort.

Wagner believed that most of our soldiers were "simulators," young men who simply were afraid to return to the front and had found a way of avoiding their obligations in the formation of willed hysterical symptoms. He considered them malingerers, liars and cowards.

Neither Wagner nor the political authorities apparently considered it reasonable that young men who had been exposed to the horrors of war might have suffered severe psychological traumas that could have prevented their further participation in the war effort. Nor did they seem troubled that these young men had symptoms that hypochondriacs would have been unable to imitate. It is just not possible to "will" a paralysis of the arm or leg.

But in wartime reasons of State represent a deep moral

obligation that, so the authorities and Wagner agreed, out-weigh any private considerations, including self-preserva-tion in the face of horrors that neither Wagner nor any of our political leaders had ever seen firsthand. We build stat-ues to our great generals, forgetting that it is the ordinary soldier who has suffered and sacrificed most in bringing glory to the State. We call "courageous" political leaders who send our young men to war, without ever asking our-selves what courage these men show in sacrificing the lives of others.

Psychoanalysis has tried to explain the psychological rea-sons for our acceptance of this moral authority. But Wagner's "liars" and "malingerers" challenged that moral authority—and, I must now add, psychoanalytic explana-tions as well—in ways that I could not at the time explain.

Wagner didn't see any moral challenge in these young men. On the contrary, since they were "simulators"—a euphemism for "liars"—they were faking illness; the treat-ment of choice was to beat the lies out of them. Medical practice became an ally to the police department. Even the innocent confess and plead guilty, so why wouldn't the young men of the Austrian army correct their ways? And he found his most perfect collaborator in the person of Michael Kozlowski.

The "malingerers" were placed in tiny cells, where they were isolated for several days. With much fanfare a young man was yanked from a cell, stripped and tied to a chair. Addressing himself to those still locked in their cells, Kozlowski "prepared" his victims with a loud warning,

"You don't know what you're in for," and then proceeded
to apply strong electric currents to the most sensitive areas
of the victim tied to the chair, shouting at him, *"Now
you'll pay for what you've done!"*

Word did get out about the "treatments" and some
families complained to Wagner, who reassured them saying
that he didn't have time to administer the treatments himself, but that the clinic used the most advanced scientific
techniques, and that he would certainly look into the matter of any abuses on the part of his assistants. He then
wrote to the families saying that any reports of torture
were totally unfounded. The families of the brutalized
young men accepted Wagner's assurances and joined forces
with him, insisting that their sons return to the front. The
Austrian government had no end of praise for Wagner's
miraculous cures.

But when the war was over some young men had second thoughts about Wagner's clinic. The story broke into
the newspapers and soon all Vienna was asking if Wagner
had tortured our young men.[1] The army was forced to

---

[1] Typical of the comments that appeared in the newspapers at
the time are the following from an article in *Der Freie Soldat* (*The
Free Soldier*) on February 28th, 1919: "[The soldiers] were
accused of malingering from the outset, and many so-called doc-
tors were concerned with 'unmasking' them, not with diagnosing
or curing their illness. One of the methods used was treatment
with electric power currents. . . . This method was used particularly at the Wagner-Jaurreg clinic. . . . Exactly after the manner of
medieval torturers, Professor Wagner's assistant, Dr. Kozlowski,
first threatened [an officer] with faradization, then made him

make an inquiry into the clinic's activities and I was asked
to be an expert witness. This was Wagner's "trial."[2]
   But let me return for a moment to the Hellbach affair.

---

watch wretched victims of electrical treament twisting and howl-
ing with pain, and finally subjected him to this agony himself" (in
K. R. Eissler, *Freud as an Expert Witness,* trans. Christine
Trollope, New York: International Universities Press, 1986).

   [2] At this point in the *Manuscript* Freud apparently began a new
train of thought that he quickly abandoned. The following passage at the end of the chapter was crossed out by Freud: The
State can easily justify itself: it gives you your identity (Austrian,
German, French, etc.) and protects you. Surely if the State has
created you, has made you feel a person of worth ("I am from
Berlin," you will proudly announce when touring Russia), it has
the right to destroy you as well. The State's relation to its citizens
is not very different from Dr. Frankenstein's to his robot. Mary
Shelley's book is, in part, about the psychology of murder and
war. We justify our cruelest acts by telling ourselves we are only
destroying what *we* have created.

4. The Obituary

*H*ellbach's trial, as I have already mentioned, became
a national pastime in Austria, followed with the
same zeal as the battles of the Great War. Those patriots
who had never questioned the government's wartime decisions now spoke of the incompetence of the judicial system,
the medical profession and the politicians. None of this was
foreign to my own thinking, but I found it extraordinary
that the real culprit was never mentioned either in the press
or in the coffeehouse debates—my fellow medical student,
colleague, Nobel Prize winner and Austria's most famous
and prestigious scientist and psychologist, Julius Wagner-
Jaurreg. Wagner never made any public, or to my knowledge private, statements about the Hellbach affair and the
press failed to mention that Michael Kozlowski, the author
of Innocent but Guilty, the book that was at the center of
the scandal and the reason Kozlowski had become the bête
noire of the Hellbach affair, had been Wagner's closest
associate. The significance of Wagner's silence only became
evident to me when a friend of mine, who had recently
returned from Kraków, showed me an obituary of

Kozlowski that Wagner had written and that had been published in a Polish magazine.

It was then that I came to understand the importance of these events for me: they related to the deepest humiliation of my life, which occurred during the trial not of Hellbach, but during that other "trial," this one ostensibly of my old friend, Julius Wagner—though I wonder if it wasn't my trial as much as his. It was upon reading Wagner's obituary of Kozlowski that I began to understand what had happened to me in 1920.

"My relations with Doctor Kozlowski," Wagner wrote in his obituary, "became a deep friendship, based on his medical experience, his absolute loyalty, his profound sense of duty and his sincere devotion to me."[1] And if so, I wondered, why hadn't Wagner published this in German? Why hadn't he come to the defense of his "friend" and colleague now, when Kozlowski, who could no longer come to his own defense, was being vilified by the Austrian press?

My concern in 1935 was hardly neutral. In 1920 Kozlowski, writing from Kraków, had treated me and my work with a disdain that makes my blood run cold to this day. And he had acted with the full accord and approval of Wagner.

But I had accepted my humiliation in 1920 because, at the time, I had felt that I hadn't deserved better. I had

---

[1] *Polska Gazeta Lekarska*, 14:323. (See Eissler, *op. cit.,* p. 129, for full letter in English.)

failed, I had thought, because of the inadequacy of my own work.

Future biographers, I suspect, will be surprised to learn that the events of 1920 drove me into one of the most severe depressions of my life, a depression from which I recovered only when I had completely forgotten Wagner's trial and my extraordinary feeling of failure. My writing in those years reflects more than I would want to admit just how successfully I had repressed anything to do with Wagner and his trial.

So if I saw in Wagner's silence about the Hellbach affair a cowardly retreat and I found the publication of his obituary of Kozlowski in Polish an attempt to keep his own role in these events quiet, he nonetheless reminded me of my own inability to confront my failure and subsequent humiliation in 1920.

In 1935 I could no longer criticize Wagner because I too had been guilty of cowardice. I knew Wagner had been wrong, had won an international reputation for work that would have better been ignored and that had, already in 1935, less than ten years after his Nobel Prize, fallen into a well-deserved oblivion. But none of this could have justified my own actions in 1920.

Wagner's obituary has awakened these painful events in me and now for the first time I can begin to understand what it was that I had failed to say during the 1920 "trial." I no longer have the time to give a full account of what I know I should have argued, but I must content myself with a sketchy outline of my present thoughts.

5. The Inquiry

I can still remember the enormous pleasure I had
when I had received the invitation to testify at the
military inquiry.[1] All the years of hostility were now a
thing of the past.

I have never before written of the events of 1920, for in
truth they created a very short-lived illusion that I was
among those scientists to whom a great nation like Austria
was ready to listen. A few years ago, in 1929, I had a similar illusion, at that time regarding the German nation,
when Thomas Mann found a place for me in the history of
modern thought and a year later my daughter Anna
received, as my proxy, in the Rathaus of Frankfort-am-
Main, the Goethe Prize for 1930. The German people
have since turned their backs on us and certainly it would
be wrong for me to see in this any personal affront, as
Germany is presently in the grip of a destructive movement
that bodes ill for all of mankind.

---

[1] Freud also refers to the "military inquiry" as "Wagner's
'trial.' "

But in 1920 we were recovering from the war and the tragic death of my sister's son. I was emotionally and physically exhausted and consequently little prepared to continue fighting for the acceptance of the new science of psychoanalysis. Vienna had always been particularly unreceptive to my work and it was therefore a pleasant surprise for me to have been asked to be an expert witness at the army inquest about Wagner's clinic.

Of course I should have known what awaited me; it should have been perfectly obvious to me that there was no reason for those who had rejected psychoanalysis to have altered their views; men change their opinions when there is some obvious personal advantage. In 1920 psychoanalysis offered nothing more than the excitement of a new science and the scorn of the establishment. Hence my naïveté in believing that the invitation to take part in the inquiry meant that my work, abused by the medical establishment for nearly two decades, was finally being recognized officially, and that the years of hostility from the medical profession and the popular press were now a thing of the past.

Indeed, my elation was such that though Wagner, whom, as I have said, I had known since my days in medical school, had never expressed a kind word about my work, I felt no particular hostility toward him, nor desire for revenge; I was not anxious to be overly critical of my friend. On the contrary, I was prepared to limit whatever criticisms I might have to purely technical matters. Wagner and I had maintained a courteous, indeed friendly, *exchange of letters throughout the years since our studies together.*

Nonetheless, when I examined the complaints against Wagner, I could not escape the conclusion that he had been guilty of gravely unethical behavior; his "cure" was putting medicine in the service of the State. The Austrian government needed men at the front; by any means at his disposal Wagner was prepared to fulfill that requirement. The primary concerns of Wagner's clinic were not medical, but political and military expediency. And while I certainly had deep misgivings about Wagner's understanding of human psychology, I was not anxious to air our differences in public.

So I prepared a short paper in which I stated my concern that Wagner had been serving the State rather than attempting to solve a genuine medical problem and I argued that psychoanalysis had shown that symptoms such as hysterical paralysis had their origins in the affective lives of the patients.[2] It did not seem unreasonable to argue that any young man might seek to avoid military service

---

[2] In a document in which Freud does not hesitate to admit to a sweeping theoretical failure, it is surprising that he does not mention that he did not *publish* the paper he read before the Austrian commission (see below) and did not include it in his own list of his published and unpublished works. The paper was found in the Austrian Archives and was first published in English in 1955. Of course, the *Manuscript* gives us ample reasons for Freud's desire to leave this paper in what he earlier calls "the scrap heap of past stupidities"; it is unclear if he believes the paper no longer exists, or cannot bring himself to discuss his desire to suppress it.

*because of the horrors of the battlefield and the brutal,
repressive regimen of the military.*

*While concluding that it was possible one might attempt
to avoid service by simulating various diseases, I argued,
contrary to the views of Wagner and his associates, there
were, in fact, very few "simulators," if for no other reason
than that it is very difficult to simulate any disease.
Furthermore, I offered the view that the fulfillment of
their military duties, far from being something to avoid,
was in fact vital to the self-esteem of these men. Indeed,
soldiers who developed war neuroses had, I argued, suffered unconscious conflicts between the desire to flee and
the desire to return to the front and win honor for themselves. This conflict was at the root of their War Neuroses
that I believed could not be cured by electric therapy.*

*It was at best a mild attack on Wagner. But Wagner and
the commission of inquiry ultimately rejected my arguments.[3] They insisted that any psychoanalytic treatment*

---

[3] Ernest Jones noted that Wagner had resented Freud's paper:
"Freud's friendliness," Jones wrote, "was by no means reciprocated.
One would have thought that he had been generous enough in his
Memorandum, more so than a stranger would have been, but
Wagner-Jaurreg was not satisfied. When he wrote his autobiography,
published posthumously . . . he not only accused Freud of intoler-
ance, but maintained that out of revenge for the criticisms emanat-
ing from the Psychiatric Clinic [that is, criticisms of Freud] he
instituted . . . a personal attack on Wagner-Jaurreg. . . . Not content
with that, Wagner-Jaurreg perpetuated the legend . . . that Janet was
the true father of psychoanalysis" (Jones, *op. cit.*, vol. II, p. 24).

would take too long, given the priority of sending the young men back to the front as soon as possible.

In the days following my presentation, much of the committee's time was spent attacking psychoanalytic theory. I was not present at these proceedings.

In the end Wagner was exonerated and the story was quickly forgotten by the press. The young men who had brought charges against Wagner were admonished and psychoanalysis was again dismissed as a foolish fraud. I was devastated in the following weeks, having gone from a feeling of euphoria that I was finally being recognized by my colleagues to the deep sense that I had been invited by the board to be humiliated.

I tried to put the whole experience behind me, though looking back I now know why I felt so defenseless and humiliated. In the course of the commission's investigation it became obvious to me that I had been set up. The army and the medical establishment had invited me as an "expert" witness who, they must have been sure, would oppose Wagner (and perhaps as a friend they expected my criticism to be mild). Yet, since my work was held in such low esteem by the medical profession, however reasonable my criticisms might have been, one and all alike would be so prejudiced against anything I might have to say that my remarks would be dismissed without any careful consideration of their worth.

I had hoped, before giving my testimony at the inquiry, that, though I could easily have delivered a devastating criticism of Wagner's practice during the war, my obvious *desire to avoid any harsh remarks might have won approval from the establishment and in the long run won new adherents to psychoanalysis. If I was naive, if I had been duped and used by the medical and political establishment, if I felt deeply humiliated by the entire affair, today I know that I deserved just what I got. For I had believed that my arguments were superior to Wagner's, that my ethics stood well above his.*

Today I know that I had invited my own humiliation; the challenge I threw down to the commission of inquiry was not only mild; it was no better than what Wagner had argued. Indeed both Wagner and I had presented arguments that were morally, if not medically, reprehensible.

6. Paralysis

*I*t is certainly no accident that I completed my book
Group Psychology *shortly after the inquiry and, subse-*
quently, my attempt to explain the origins of our moral
sense in The Ego and the Id.[1] *Political questions and their*
relation to my theory of psychoanalysis had begun to
obsess me and—as psychoanalysis had demonstrated—like
all obsessions, mine were not devoid of paranoia and a
deep sense of guilt. I was suspicious of the motives of
those who had invited me to testify; but I was also guilty
over my failure to adequately defend the young men who
had been tortured, so I believed, under Wagner's aegis. I
was now desperately seeking to correct the wrong I had
done, my abandonment of those young men and my con-
sequent failure to have left my mark on the judges and in
the public mind. I became obsessed with redoing my past,
correcting it, succeeding where I had all too ignominiously

[1] *Group Psychology and the Analysis of the Ego* was originally
published in German in 1920. The first English edition
appeared in 1922 (SE 18:69). *The Ego and the Id* was published
in German in 1923. The first English edition was published in
1925 (SE 19:3).

failed; I wrote obsessively about the psychological roots of morality.

My brief statement that medicine must be independent of political authority had been lost on the commission in 1920 because I had failed to give it due emphasis out of concern for my friend Wagner. It is only now that I am able to admit to myself that this concern was never acknowledged or appreciated by Wagner; and it is only now that I can understand it was a concern that stemmed from my own feeling of inadequacy. I too was cowed by Wagner's reputation; and my desire was not so much to criticize him as to win his respect and recognition for what I had created. But Wagner took offense at my ever-so-mild criticism and for all these years I have not understood why. I have had to put the blame on myself and today I can frankly acknowledge that if I was, at the time, intimidated by Wagner and the commission, it was because I was unable to back up my moral attack with any psychological theory.

In my obsessive attempts to come to grips with these cataclysmic events in my life I wrote that the moral force of our leaders derived from a psychology that was not moral in any true sense of the term. I had argued that the sons' desires, real or imagined, to kill the father, had given rise to a pervading sense of guilt from which the sons could not liberate themselves. This was the basis of moral authority.

In the back of my mind I must have constantly been asking myself about the young men that Wagner had called "simulators" and who had been tortured by him. The more I wrote about our sense of guilt, the more I was becoming aware that I was leaving unexplained what I had failed to explain to the commission in 1920. In fact, the real challenge to moral authority—and to psychoanalytic theory—was those young men.

What I had misunderstood at the time was the psychology of the young men whom Wagner saw fit to torture. I had suggested that their neuroses could have been "cured" through psychoanalysis since these neuroses were the consequence of unconscious affective conflicts. But this was to replace Wagner's torture sessions with a "talking" cure. I was as prepared as Wagner to send these young men back to the front, and consequently my criticism of Wagner lost its force.

Indeed, I had overlooked an important clue about our psychological structure. The young men who had developed paralyses were refusing to accept the madness of the State.[2] There was no way they could argue against the State, no way they could justify their fears, because there was no social protest of any importance. They had been abandoned by every "moral" authority.

---

[2] This too is entirely unprecedented in Freudian thought. A vaguely similar idea was hinted at as early as 1897 when Freud wrote to Fliess, "[W]ith the successive waves of a child's development, he is overlaid with piety, shame, and such things, . . . [and] the non-occurrence of this extinction of the sexual zones can produce moral insanity" (Letter 71, in SE 1:270; the words "moral insanity" are in English in the original letter). Of course, in the *Manuscript* sexual development is no longer the issue. It is the madness of authority that causes psychological and physical paralysis.

Yet after their experiences at the front they could not justify, at least to themselves, the State's claims to moral authority; nor could they reject the State. They had been abandoned by medicine, science and their families. Indeed, they had nowhere to turn and yet they had a deep sense of fear not just out of a need for self-preservation, but their almost instinctive understanding that there was something absurd and unjustifiable about the circumstances in which they had been placed. And yet they were unable to articulate what it was that was troubling them, because there was no social or familial structure that understood or assisted them. They were afraid of something that neither they nor anyone else seemed to understand; and their reaction was the only appropriate one in the circumstances: they became physically paralyzed. Their paralysis was both a symbolic reaction to circumstances beyond anyone's control and a very real solution to a fundamentally hopeless bind.

But, we may ask ourselves, what psychological mechanisms could be responsible for this paralysis? What strikes us immediately is that these young men are no longer capable of self-deception; they are no longer able to deceive themselves either about their status in society— they can no longer accept the role of the "hero" or the "patriot"—nor can they deceive themselves about their ability to convince others that the world is an irrational place. They can no longer accept the State or any other authority, because accepting authority is a form of self-deception. Authority, the State, pretends to know all, to have universal understanding, which these young men have, without necessarily being able to articulate these ideas, now come to recognize as a hollow claim.

We are here at the frontier between the physical and the mental and future research will have to tell us why the loss of self-deception causes paralysis. I am sure that there is much variation among individuals, but I would not be surprised to learn that it is the inability of these young men to continue being deceived by their emotions and their consequent inability to articulate their own morality that is at the heart of the matter.[3]

---

[3] The "hysterical" paralysis of these young men is a rather spectacular confirmation of the view that emotions normally disguise the irrationality of our actions—in other words, that emotions are at the heart of our self-deception. See Freud's earlier discussion of the role of emotions in self-deception, p. 66. See too p. 66, Footnote 8, for a reference about Frontal Lobe Syndromes in which the loss of affect (emotions) causes an inability to act (paralysis).

7. An Outdated Morality

*B*ut in 1920 my concern was more with my own relation to Austrian society. If I had believed that I had
been invited to testify because the importance of my work
was now being recognized, I very soon learned of my own
self-deception. I had been but a pawn in the hands of
Wagner and his associates. I was unable to confront my
failure, a failure that was intellectual as well as personal,
and I spent the next decade obsessed by the problem of
authority, never once realizing that psychoanalytic theory
was deeply flawed.

In 1928 Julius Wagner received the Nobel Prize for
Malaria Therapy. Now, less than a decade later, Wagner's
great cure for syphilitic paralysis is all but forgotten.[1]

---

[1] Freud had added the following phrase after the word "forgotten" that was later crossed out: "and this is perhaps the best
comment I could make about the significance of prizes that carry
great prestige and that have become an obsession among members of the scientific, if not literary, community in our own day."
On the same page in the margin of Bernadette Schilder's copy of
the *Manuscript* Freud wrote and crossed out the following paragraph:

*Wagner's "theory" was to replace one disease by another—
an idea that the Nobel Committee apparently didn't know
goes back to Hippocrates if not before. Patients who were
paralyzed by syphilis, were "cured" of their paralyses when
they were infected with malaria. Of course, Wagner had
only replaced one form of suffering with another and had
certainly not extended the life spans of his patients. But
then Wagner's "cure" was no different from the "cure" he
had proposed for the hysterical paralyses of the young
Austrian soldiers. Violence (electric therapy) made them
return to the front, just as violence (a good dose of malaria)
made the paralyzed syphilitic walk again. In some sense Wagner must have considered all forms of disease "simulation."*

Once crowned with the glory of a Nobel Prize, both
Malaria Therapy and Wagner became untouchable. Men
who had doubts before never uttered a word of protest after
the Nobel Committee elected Wagner and his therapy to
the rank of the "immortals." But has anyone asked why a
man who invented dynamite, who sought his own form of
immortality in creating an expensive prize, should have so
great an influence on the thoughts of reasonable men?
Reputations are created overnight, and it is perhaps the ease
with which this is possible, and the extraordinary status of
the prize holders, that has created a new obsession for
prizes. Ordinary obsessives one day become geniuses the
next. I find more curious not the foolish elevation of these
men to a status that has nothing to do with their worth, but
their apparent belief that they indeed merit all the attention
and admiration they have received. Worse still, they crave
even greater acclaim once they find themselves so venerated.
Of course, my own experience has been limited to a Looker
Laureate, Norman Dicke. Nonetheless, everything Freud says
about Wagner and the Nobel Prize is true of Dicke as well.

At the time I was upset that Wagner was being given this recognition because I believed it was I who truly deserved it. I too had argued that my patients were replacing one form of disease (neurosis) for another, but I thought that my arguments about psychology were, if nothing else, more subtle, revealing and ultimately far more important than Wagner's.[2]

What was perhaps most disturbing to me in the weeks and months following Wagner's exoneration was that I had to admit that we had strikingly similar views about morality. I had still not understood the challenge of our young Austrian soldiers. Both Wagner and I, each in his own way, had accepted the idea that there were deep psychological reasons for our acceptance of authority figures. Neither of us was at all troubled by the underlying morality that the authority might represent. It seemed irrelevant.

I had tried to overcome this lack of moral content by postulating that our respect for authority derives from a sense of guilt, that there was a true or an imagined crime, the killing of the father, that had created this sense of guilt and that was responsible for our obedience to subsequent authority figures. That we could have a sense of guilt even

---

[2] Again Freud added a comment here though he drew a thick line through it, leaving the sentence still legible: "What am I to make of that nasty story (or is it a joke?) I've heard of late that Thomas Mann nominated me for the Nobel Prize as long as it wasn't in Literature and Albert Einstein as long as it wasn't in Science (at least not physics, since medicine's not much of a science)?" The source of this story is unknown.

about imagined events meant that our actions had a moral grounding; we make distinctions between right and wrong and we judge ourselves accordingly. I thought that I had come upon a rather extraordinary connection between psychology and morality and had shown how, in spite of ourselves, our deeply moralistic nature always pervaded our thoughts and actions.

We could try to avoid our own moral commands, but we were inevitably confronted by our "guilt." Our desires to act against our better judgments might outweigh these moral commands, but even if our psyche could hide from us those judgments, we would always confront an unexplained guilt that manifested itself, often enough as a vague feeling of dissatisfaction.[3]

In Wagner's view, however, even guilt was not necessary—we are what we appear to be. Men are either honest or liars. The theory of repression was abhorrent to him

---

[3] Freud's view, it seems to me, is remarkably similar to that of the Game Theorist (see von Neumann's conversation with Anna Freud, pp. 157–158)—morality is strategy—and yet much deeper, for it attempts to explain the *need* to behave in a given way. We are, Freud says, *driven* by our *feelings* of guilt. In Game Theory, it could be argued, we are driven by the desire to win, but feelings are not necessary. The whole process can be programmed on a computer and, of course, the ultimate "biological" entity, so dear to the biologist using Game Theory, is the Selfish Gene, which certainly has no feelings to speak of. A Freudian robot, on the other hand, would manifest its moral qualms by *feeling guilty*—though just what a robot capable of guilt would be like is well beyond present-day technological developments. Yet, however deep Freud's views might be, he rejects them in the following chapter.

because it suggested that we might say things that are not true—our recollections might be inaccurate—while believing we are telling the truth. The idea that we might want to be honest and, in spite of ourselves, could not be, was a morally reprehensible idea for Wagner—and hence psychologically impossible. The notions of "right" and "wrong" were, for Wagner, perfectly self-evident, lacking in any ambiguity and without any need for doubt. Like my teachers at the end of the past century, Wagner's limited view of morality determined his ideas about human psychology.

Whatever the limitations of my theory of repression, it was conceived as an answer to these simple-minded ideas about psychology and morality. For I understood that at the root of Wagner's psychology was a very rigid, conformist set of ideas about morality; his theory of psychology, as I said, derived from his morality.

It was thus that I decided to reverse the equation, to demonstrate the complex ambiguities of our psychologies and to show that our social rules—even our notions of "right" and "wrong"—are, in part at least, the consequence of those ambiguities. Just as the solar system model of the atom gave the physicists an important first step into understanding the interior of the atom—a model that they have since abandoned—so my theory of repression gave me an important initial understanding of how to relate psychological ambiguities and morality.

In Wagner's view, however, there was an unspecified assumption that those in power had the right to call for our obedience. This was a question of blind belief, since "patriotism" needed no justifications. In the end, this explained his treatment of our soldiers and his Nobel Prize–winning treatment of the paralyzed syphilitic. Often enough these cures didn't last very long and this only reinforced the need for further brutality.

If Wagner's Nobel Prize had deeply disturbed me, it failed, nonetheless, to shake my conviction that at the root of morality was a sense of guilt. Perhaps it reinforced this conviction, because it gave me a sense that my argument was more subtle—and more moral—than Wagner's. Yet the more I tried to deepen my ideas about morality and psychology, the more I found myself going around in circles.

It was only when I asked myself about the psychology of the leader that I suddenly saw where I had gone wrong. It was only then that I realized it had been odd for me to talk about morality without ever asking myself about the authorities themselves. I had never asked myself if there were any justifications for the ambivalence toward authority—even the desire to kill—that I had so often observed in the neurotic personality.

Psychoanalysis had always been but a first step toward understanding the human psyche. If, as I knew would be inevitable, psychoanalysis was to one day be replaced by a better and more complete theory, it would not be possible until the discoveries we had made, and the theoretical advances that had come from those discoveries, were first given a firm grounding. I never hesitated, when new discoveries required, to revise fundamental ideas in psychoanalytic theory. But I have been confronted with a hostile *medical profession and an equally hostile public that has not simplified my task. I have had to defend our accomplishments and this has taken valuable time from my work in advancing the theory. Inevitably, I concentrated my efforts on those areas where we had our greatest successes, the neuroses. In my clinic I saw patients who were deeply troubled by authority figures; but I never saw the authorities themselves. This was a failing that I can only now begin to overcome.*

8. Megalomania

I

I was rereading the proofs of my book Der Mann Moses
und die Monotheistische Religion *when suddenly everything fell into place—my obsession with Moses for more
than four decades, my inability to confront my humiliation
and failure before the Austrian commission in 1920 and
Wagner's denial of his role in the Hellbach trial that was
revealed in his publishing only in Polish an obituary of his
friend and colleague Kozlowski.*

I saw what I had failed to grasp. What came to me is this:
**Authority is by its very nature psychotic—and this is a
form of megalomania.**[1] *It is psychotic because it claims to
have a global understanding of the world and because as a
consequence of that claim it cannot tolerate any criticism,
however trivial. It is psychotic because its ultimate defense of
its own authority is violence, since given its global and
unique understanding, no other individual can share its
views or fully understand the basis of its authority; and it is*

---

[1] Perhaps not unsurprisingly, some of those who read the
Manuscript when it was circulated for comments before publication reacted specifically to Freud's claim that authority is psychotic. For a selection of comments, see the Endnotes, pp. 168–169.

psychotic because it is based on an illusory set of ideas that combine often intentionally obscure and incomprehensible arguments with banalities that are taken, unacknowledged, from the works of others. Its obscurantism is justified because of the global understanding of the psychotic (mega-lomaniac)—only he is privy to the true understanding of the world.

Law is our oldest and most durable example of a psychot-ic's (megalomaniac's) works: it is absolute, all-knowing (it determines the nature of knowledge and of right and wrong), arbitrary and obscure (hence the need for lawyers, judges and the whole of the legal apparatus).

It is hardly surprising that psychoanalysis discovered an ambivalent and often undirected sense of guilt in its neu-rotic patients. But we have not done our patients justice, because we have not understood the true significance of the ambivalence.[2]

II

It is true that I had always thought of Julius Wagner as an old school comrade.[3] *In the years following medical school*

---

[2] Thomas Szasz summed up some of these ideas in 1974 when he wrote, "Doubt is to certainty as neurosis is to psychosis. The neurotic is in doubt and he fears about persons and things; the psychotic has convictions and makes claims about them. In short the neurotic has problems, the psychotic has solutions" (Thomas Szasz, *The Age Of Madness*, 1974).

[3] The following part of Chapter 8 of the *Manuscript* shows Freud's partial revisions. The marginal comments in Bernadette

*I was beginning to develop my ideas that eventually
became the core of psychoanalytic theory. Wagner had little interest in my work and I never insisted. I was, in truth,
as I have said, intimidated by him. I was ashamed to tell
him the broad outlines of my thinking because I feared
that he would reject my ideas; and I feared him because he
had a self-assurance that I found devastating. He appeared
to me to be someone who knew what was right and what
was wrong and my ideas were too incoherent for me to
present them to him with any confidence. Wagner was one
of those men whose self-confidence, whose cynical disre-
gard for the thoughts and feelings of others instilled in you
a respect for him that knew no bounds.*

Schilder's copy cannot be fully deciphered and I have thought it
wiser not to speculate on how he might have rewritten this chapter if he had had more time. In general he appears to have had
certain misgivings concerning the comparison between Hellbach
and Wagner. I have decided to give the entire chapter here, for it
does forcefully portray Freud's view of the megalomanical personality, a view to which recent clinical studies have given powerful
support. (See, for example, John Young *et al.*, "The physiological
basis of the 'megalomanical' personality: inhibitory mechanisms
in the temporal cortex," *Proceedings of the National Academy of
Sciences* 45 (1998), pp. 2341–2447. Also see Bernard Held,
"Prozac and Personality Changes," *The New England Journal of
Medicine* 79 (1997), pp. 220–223. SONY Labs in Tokyo has produced some interesting experiments that are recorded in, "A
robot that thinks about itself," *Robotics* 3 (1999), pp. 25–41.

Bernadette Schilder agreed that it was best to keep this chapter. She said it reminded her of an important scientist she had met
not very long ago. And, of course, as the reader will no doubt
notice himself, there is something of Dicke, as I have described
him in my introduction, that Freud has captured too.

*But then when all Vienna was talking about the rapist and
Kozlowski's book, my friend showed me Wagner's obituary
of his former colleague. I had known ever since 1920 that
Wagner and Kozlowski had worked closely together.
Kozlowski hadn't been present at the inquiry, but he had
sent a letter in defense of Wagner explaining that he had
never tortured any soldier, but on the contrary had spent
most of his time treating patients through suggestion rather
than actual use of electric currents. "You must understand,"
he wrote to the commission, "that the method we were
using—a method that was both physically and morally trying for the physician— was associated with techniques that
did not use any electrical currents." He noted that he had
threatened an exhibitionist who was manifestly incorrigible
with electrical therapy, but that he had never in fact used the
electrodes on him. He described his menacing words in
front of the cells of the imprisoned soldiers as "a bit of suggestion to tell the impostors that they would be submitted
to something mysterious and very efficacious." And he was
proud of having sent back to the front many an "impostor"
who, following his mild electrical therapy, suddenly was able
to walk and carry out his duties as any other honorable soldier in the army. Indeed, many a simulator thanked him for
his treatment and returned to the front, where he fought
and died with honor.*[4]

Kozlowski's failure to be present at the commission's

---

[4] The full letter can be found in Eissler, *op. cit.* Appendix 5, pp.
390–395.

inquiry was, I had thought at the time, suspect. And his letter was, according to all witnesses at the inquiry, a tissue of lies. But Wagner stood by his former colleague. At the time, I found this admirable—until I saw his obituary of Kozlowski in Polish and noted his silence about the trial of Hellbach.

But why all this concern with a rapist? What was it that had attracted Kozlowski to write a book about him and to solicit the support of Wagner in winning a reprieve for him? As I became more interested in the trial, the rapist became a personality that began to fascinate me and I began to have a sense of why Wagner and Kozlowski had been so interested in him.

The newspaper reports suggested a man who believed that he had a higher knowledge that ordinary mortals could not possibly possess. He disregarded the accusations against him, much as Kozlowski (and Wagner too) had disregarded the accusations of the tortured soldiers. He was following a higher and misunderstood morality.

The rapist told the court, "Whether or not my accusers have been raped I cannot say. I was too far away. Gentlemen, the facts of this case do not concern me; but having patiently listened to the charges, I too can only condemn whoever might have committed these crimes." [5]

---

[5] Luc Tangorre, the French rapist mentioned earlier (see pp. 69 and 72), declared in court, "*La réalité des viols, ce n'est past mon problème. La réalité des faits, ça ne me concerne pas*" ("The reality of the rapes is not my problem. The reality of the facts does

Like Kozlowski, and ultimately, as I learned more about a side of Wagner I had never known, like Wagner too, the rapist never spoke as if he were the accused, but as if he were the lawyer for the accused. All three men, I was beginning to understand, had succeeded in creating larger-than-life images of themselves, enormous balloons in their own image that never left their grasp, but that others envied, hated, berated and ostracized. Their egos had become these balloonlike extensions that never separated from the master, inflated caricatures of themselves.

They were able to establish themselves as higher moral authorities, above any mundane proceedings or judgments. More and more I recognized a phrase that I had heard from some of my patients and that I had always considered an acknowledgment of guilt. The rapist, Kozlowski and Wagner were constantly denying what they had said: "I never said that" was a regular refrain of these men.

What was extraordinary about this was not that it was a confession of guilt, as I had supposed in my patients, but, on the contrary, a statement that they were above all judg-

---

not concern me"). After reading the charges against him he said, "*Après avoir lu un réquisitoire qui est accablant, moi le premier je condamnerais celui qui est concerné. Mais ces éléments ne correspondent pas à la réalité*" ("After having read the charges [indictment] that are overwhelming, I would be the first to condemn whoever is concerned. But these elements do not correspond to any reality"; *Le Monde*, "Luc Tangorre s'estime victime d'une manipulation" ["Luc Tangorre considers himself a victim of manipulation"] 5 *février* 1992, p. 13).

ments of other mortals. The rapist never told anyone he
raped. He condemned it as an atrocious crime, as Wagner
and Kozlowski condemned using electric therapy for torture. And yet the one raped and the others tortured. And
none of them considered themselves guilty. The rapist
never thought of himself as a rapist any more than Wagner
or Kozlowski thought of themselves as torturers.

My patients would have been all too happy to have cried
out their guilt. No wonder analytic cures have become inter-
minable. I have raised guilt and self-flagellation to cardinal
virtues. But the rapist, Kozlowski and Wagner could never
have submitted to any form of analysis.

There was an odd relation here that analytic theory had
failed to capture, a relation of violence, extraordinary
overblown egos that had global understandings of the
world and cold-blooded lying. I was beginning to believe
that it was only if I could understand this relation that I
would finally succeed in understanding the psychological
roots of morality.

As my friend who had shown me Wagner's obituary of
Kozlowski told me more about Wagner, a strange parallel
between Wagner and the rapist began to take shape in my
mind. No one, intimate friends, colleagues and associates,
knew anything about either of them. And the little that
they might have thought they had known was certainly
not true.

Wagner, my friend told me, had always been proud of his
ability to carry out projects in utmost secrecy. He consid-

ered himself an expert in the art of creating decoys and often, during the Great War, he had imagined himself as a first-rate spy. In the past few years he has found Al Capone more to his taste as a scientific investigator. Ever since his Nobel Prize he has claimed that all his activities are part of his scientific investigations. Former colleagues tell of late-night meetings in coffeehouses where he would recount his latest scientific ideas.

And then he would leave in the early hours of the morning, saying that his wife would be very upset when he walked in at four in the morning, but he had to return to the laboratory to work. He would watch his colleague disappear up the street. Of course, many of his colleagues suspected he was visiting a mistress, which, no doubt, was an impression that Wagner was trying to create. But he was going neither to his laboratory nor to a mistress. Wagner has not lived with his wife for years. He pays her weekly unannounced visits.

He was in fact going home to a little garret that he now keeps near his clinic in Vienna. There he is surrounded by pictures of himself. In several photos he can be seen shaking hands with the Swedish king or dancing with the king's wife and other women of Swedish court. He can spend hours mesmerized by these images of himself. From time to time he looks at himself in one of the mirrors that surround him on the walls of his garret and he slips on one of his wigs that are carefully stored in his drawer, covering the bald spot on his head. Even in his medical school days

Wagner would tap the top of his bald head as he spoke and then push up the tip of his nose with his index finger.[6]

Whatever Wagner did, I believe, he thought of as transcending normal human capacities. His evasive tactics were a sign of his exceptional nature and compelled, he thought, admiration. Of course, given the extraordinary nature of his work that would merit more prizes in the future and a place in the pantheon of the greatest minds of all time, he had to be wary of those who sought to steal and plagiarize his thoughts. He was careful in what he said as he was careful in what he committed to paper. This lent a clandestine air to all his activities that many misunderstood.

And it was this extraordinary nature that excused whatever minor flaws of character he might from time to time exhibit. He had a right to such flaws; ordinary men had the flaws and nothing else. And this is why he had the right, and indeed the obligation, to direct the activities of others—for their own good, as well as that of the public.

Hellbach had, in his own way, succeeded at this game brilliantly. He had been arrested for rape and then exonerated by the president of the Republic. He too could not believe that anyone could see through his diversionary tactics. What the Nobel Prize was for Wagner, the exoneration of the president of the Republic was for Hellbach. They had been recognized by the most important authorities in the world.

---

[6] It is not clear if the source of Freud's remarks is his "friend" or if Freud is taking certain liberties here, largely extrapolating from his recollections of Wagner during their days together in medical school.

And those who challenged Wagner, or Hellbach, had to be destroyed, as nations destroy those who challenge their power. They were violent toward, and intolerant of, all who failed to admire them. At the heart of their success was their ability to deceive, but neither they nor those who admired them ever expressed this idea.

But the respect and admiration that a Wagner or a Hellbach could command was inevitably limited in time. Ordinary minds would eventually think that they could do what a Wagner had done, never once understanding that every thought they had ever had was because of Wagner. When they were devoted to him they absorbed his way of thought, his genius and then they would forget the sources of their ideas. They would lie and cheat. Wagner and Hellbach couldn't lie, because they had perfected the art of lying to a point where truth had become unrecognizable. They had so consistently lied, and won praise for their lies and deceptions, that they created within their own minds a view of the world that only they could be privy to.

These men were constantly revealing themselves in "sacred texts" (Wagner's "theory" and its later additions, Hellbach's comments recorded by journalists), creating new conundrums. Inconsistencies showed the limited understanding of others, for inconsistencies, even blatant contradictions, would disappear once the whole could be grasped. Sure Wagner appeared to lie, cheat and steal, as Hellbach appeared to rape.

It was Wagner who was often quoted as saying, "I

haven't lied and cheated all my life to have some little bastard like that steal the show."

He had said that because there was no way ordinary mortals could understand what he was talking about. When a policeman pretends he is a faithful member of a gang of thieves in order to trap them, is he lying and cheating? Or is he helping maintain the social order? He has a higher purpose that the members of the gang can never understand.

What was extraordinary about Hellbach and Wagner was the absolute conviction with which they would proceed. These were not men who sought to deceive the world, even if deception was exactly what they were most talented at. No, Wagner and Hellbach were convinced that they had a totality of knowledge and understanding that exempted them from any judgments of ordinary mortals.

If there was one mental attribute they both lacked, it was a sense of guilt. It was this realization that has made me reconsider the sources of moral authority in the human psyche.

III

For a long time we have known that narcissism is an infantile stage of development and that this narcissism is disturbed by the admonitions of others. Psychoanalyses have shown that the child seeks to recover what I have called the "narcissistic perfection of his childhood" by creating what I formerly called an "ego ideal" and with further study I now call the superego—an incorporation into the psyche of the admonitions of parents and other authority figures. Psychoanalytic theory explains that what we call in everyday language "conscience" is this superego; and we have seen many patients who have paranoid delusions of being "watched," which is nothing more than the admonitions of their superegos.[7]

The superego, then, was what I had believed to be the

---

[7] The *Manuscript* continues here as follows:

Do men (the Wagners) make themselves into heroes, not through their own thoughts and actions, but through the misstatement of their deeds, an extraordinary overvaluation of their worth and significance by others, who being in love with their heroes and themselves (the Kozlowskis), develop "blind spots" at the expense of those who were banished from history? Kozlowski's narcissism made him prey to a very peculiar form of love, a form of hero worship in which he so overvalued his loved one, and through his loved one, himself, that he had to deny the very existence of others. Narcissism is perhaps a misnomer, for the narcissist's true value, his true love of himself, is only possible through another to whom he can attribute qualities that balance and add to his own.

The rest of the page has been badly smudged and is impossible to read. Of course, this remarkable passage brings to mind some of the most disastrous tyrannies in history that were in their early stages when Freud was writing—the Stalins and Berias, the Hitlers and Speers. These tyrants had global and grandiose plans for the future and their narcissistic henchmen "forgot," rewrote the past at the expense of history's scapegoats, even after their leaders were gone.

Note that the view of narcissism in this passage differs radically from the well-known view Freud first published in his paper "On Narcissism" in 1914. The text of the *Manuscript* is consistent with Freud's 1914 paper.

agency of our moral judgments. But if our moral judgments were derived from the admonitions of authority figures, what was the source of those admonitions? What was
the nature of the rules given to children that compelled
obedience? How, in other words, did the authorities justify
their rules? And what compelled them to give us any rules
in the first place?

If I had avoided these questions in the past, or rather
never considered them, it was because I had always been
convinced that we have an inherently moral nature that
was at the core of our psychological development. My
challenge to our great moral thinkers was not that there
could not be any morality, but that on the contrary it was
part of the very fabric of our psyche and that it inevitably
created unresolvable conflicts because we also have desires
that drive us to oppose our moral nature. Our everyday
behavior reflected, I argued, our unconscious and unsatis-
factory attempts to satisfy these conflicting demands and in
the long run, I argued, the burden would be too great and
we would do violence to ourselves and others. What I had
challenged in the thinkers of the past was the idea that
morality, an absolute "good," could become a guiding
principle for behavior, because we are more than the moral
selves I believed we had acquired in childhood.

What now became clear to me was that part of our
rejection of moral rules, was our unstated recognition that
the sources of those rules that we had internalized in childhood were themselves devoid of moral content—and
worse still, a vague sense that those who made claims to

moral authority had a psychology that was very different from our own. Fear, ignorance and intimidation prevented us from examining just how different these "moral" authorities were; and the fear and intimidation worked just because we could not understand, we were ignorant of what it was about our moral masters that was so different. Of course, we were convinced, our psychology compelled us to believe, that we needed some kind of moral authority, since without it we could only imagine the chaos that would result.

I must leave for future speculation what the world will be like when the true psychological sources of our moral laws are recognized, as I believe is inevitable with the advance of knowledge. The challenges to parental and political authority will be so deep that it will certainly wreak havoc on our familial and political institutions as we know them today.

I was wrong to believe that we would one day be overwhelmed by our own sense of guilt. As we gain a greater knowledge of ourselves we will be overwhelmed, not by guilt, but by an enormous moral vacuum that may become intolerable and cause an unleashing of destructive forces that the world has never known. For the sources of our morality we must move beyond the neuroses that have for so long preoccupied me; we must now confront the roots of our morality in psychotic behavior; and the remnant of this behavior in our everyday life we find, as I have said, in our self-deception.

For when we speak of a man's "worth," his "value," we

believe, no doubt, that we are making a moral evaluation. And yet if we think about it for a moment we all know that men of worth, heads of state, men of great wealth, even men of great scientific and intellectual achievement, hardly measure up to their public reputations.

What we know, and what we dare not say, is that the worth of a man, his value, is his ability to fake it, to respond in circumstances in which his ignorance is total without revealing, for even a moment, just how ignorant he is. The study of human history reveals this as the one and only eternal truth, the source of all invention, the impulse of civilization, the rock bottom of man's greatest achievements and glories; and it is this insight that is the jagged shore on which its own ship of glory has been cast to smithereens. It is the root of human psychology, its origin, source and most mysterious well of darkness.

We have seen it often, hovered about it, but never dared plunge into its depths. None of us has been strong enough to stand up and say, "Fraud is Man." We have done our best to clothe great fraud in glory and petty fraud in crime. We have admired it from afar, and avoided too close scrutiny; we have condemned it in lesser forms. Fraud is the commerce of everyday psychology; it is the rock bottom beyond which we cannot pierce.

We have learned this not from analysis, as I had hoped, but from observing psychotic behavior in our midst.

Indeed, what we learn from this pathology is that patients who talk about "the important," "the profound," "the great questions of the day," are often greatly inflating trivial ideas. When the megalomaniac tells us that there is nothing more important than obeying such and such a rule, it is not the content of the rule that concerns him, but that it is his rule.

The development of human psychology requires the creation of the notion of "important," but it is a fragile mirage, which, when it lacks conviction, leaves us disoriented, depressed and without a sense of being. The advantage of the psychotic, of the megalomaniac, is his unshakable belief about what is important.[8] If we could all have the same certainty, our psychological equilibrium would not be subjected to so many vicissitudes.

Some psychotics, or more specifically megalomaniacs, concern themselves with the big questions. My patient Doctor Schreber never ceased to upbraid God for his mistreatment of men.[9] Others have concerns that are so trivial, and yet presented in such grandiose terms, that we can understand that it is not the content of the megalomaniac's thinking that is important to him, but his ability to create importance out of nothing.

[8] Here again note the important role of emotions in creating belief and self-deception. (See Footnote 8 on p. 66 and Footnote 3 on p. 92.)

[9] Note, for example, the following from Schreber's writings: "God really knew nothing about living men and did not need to know; consonantly with the Order of Things, He needed only to have communication with corpses" (quoted in Freud, Psychoanalytic Notes on an Autobiographical Account of a Case of Paranoia, SE 12:25, 1911).

The megalomaniac should give us pause in our everyday discourse. When we are prepared to find a subject important, when we are prepared to defend with our lives our honor, our nation or our God, we should know that we are deceiving ourselves, that what we call "human psychology" is showing its bare bones. Normally our megalomaniacal states are limited to moments. But the true megalomaniac not only is constantly preoccupied with the important questions, but they are so difficult, so obscure, so much part of his privileged domain, that no ordinary person could in any way understand them. It is this concern with the difficult and the obscure that places the megalomaniac outside of everyday society and creates a mystery around his personality.

And behind this self-importance is a deep sense of the megalomaniac's immortality, an immortality of either his person or his works. The feeling of immortality, of the eternal, we usually consider reserved to religion, but the study of megalomania reveals it as a part of everyday psychology. Megalomaniacs believe themselves to be immortal; they are extraordinarily seductive liars, totally fraudulent in their dealings with any other individual, including those they claim to be their intimate associates. They exercise an absolute tyranny—including a total control over the manner in which others talk in their presence. What is curious too is that though the fraudulent, tyrannical nature of the megalomaniac is perfectly evident, he is terribly successful in convincing the public at large of his *"genius" and other special gifts and qualities. Fraud, I might add, seems more convincing than "honesty."*

[The Chapter ends here with some indecipherable notes.]

9. The Hallucinating Superego

*M*y years of concern with the psychological roots of morality were marked by my own obsession with the person of Moses, and it is only now that I can finally understand what it is about him that has so preoccupied me. For if we examine the biblical example of Moses, we are immediately struck by a possible source of the true nature of our moral admonitions.

What we call our conscience, our sense of morality, originates in an hallucination.

The voice that gave the Ten Commandments to Moses was not, as in the case of the paranoid delusion, someone watching over him, but, on the contrary, an ally in the fight against what Moses considered the evil practices of the idol-worshiping Jews.

The particular psychological origins of the Ten Commandments in an hallucination makes us wonder why they should have ever had any moral force. Not one of his "laws" has served to guide the behavior of any society or individual. The extraordinary irrelevancy of the Ten Commandments as moral law and the equally (hypocriti-

*cal) universal approval those laws have received since time
immemorial suggest not morality, but psychotic behavior.*[1]

*The "moral" challenge that Moses presented to the
Jews was part of his larger worldview. Moses told the Jews
they were the "chosen people," suggesting that he, or the
voices that were talking to him, knew about all other "peo-
ples." Moses had a complete knowledge of the world and
only he (and his voices) were privy to that knowledge. The
Ten Commandments were the sacred text that would
reveal over time, if they were obeyed, the totality of the
world order. They could not be questioned because they*

---

[1] The theme of the megalomaniac as hero is entirely new in the
Manuscript, though Freud, by his own account, came to this con-
clusion not because of his work on Moses, as this chapter might
suggest to some readers, but rather because of the debacle of the
inquiry of 1920 that Freud has already discussed. Indeed, the
Manuscript view of Moses is apparently an afterthought. For
Freud's preoccupation with Moses goes back at least to 1914 when
he published an "anonymous" study (in his own journal *Imago*) of
Michelangelo's *Moses*. Its authorship was known to all members of
Freud's inner circle and probably suspected by many of the journal's readers. In his study Freud interprets the Michelangelo statue
as a Moses who is holding back his anger at the Jews, suggesting
that the tablets fell and broke accidentally. He was clearly thinking
of his father, who had failed to respond to an anti-Semitic attack
when he was with him as a little boy. He had considered his father
cowardly, as he apparently considered Moses cowardly. This is his
first "denial" of a people its hero—as he writes, it will be recalled,
not only at the beginning of the *Manuscript*, but in his earlier *Moses
and Monotheism*. In *Moses and Monotheism* Freud's "denial" has
made Moses into a fraud. But on further consideration he must
have found this "denial" inadequate and finally in the *Manuscript*
Moses is described as a megalomaniac.

came from the hand of an unknowable, all-knowing God—the voices that spoke to Moses. Any resistance to these laws was met with violence and Moses did not hesitate to kill the disobedient Jews.[2]

The one piece of evidence that might have given credence to Moses' claims, the stones on which he had carved the laws that had been dictated to him by his God, was "destroyed" by Moses when he smashed the tablets. It is not proof that is necessary for moral law, but self-confidence and force.

We are immediately struck by the similarity to cases of "delusions of paranoia" and we might be tempted to attribute the very same psychological mechanisms to Moses. But a little reflection tells us that these cases are very dissimilar.

Moses did not have a paranoid vision. The voice he heard was not, as I have said, watching over him. And when Moses sought advice, God willingly helped him. For Moses does not fear God; he tells the Jews that the encounter with the "All-mighty" is a "scary" experience, a claim that we might better understand if he had said, as a

[2] In an apparent comment on his own text, Freud wrote the following in the margin that he then crossed out: "I'll be accused of blasphemy for all this, but what is truly blasphemous are the pretensions of religions, to knowledge and to the right to dictate morality. After all, what is blasphemy but the arrogance of others!" Freud's view of religion that emerges from the following pages is, I believe, considerably deeper than that found in his previous writings, including his best-known work on religion, *The Future of an Illusion.*

*Wagner had, that it is scary for the ignorant to be con-
fronted with the totality of knowledge.*[3]

*The ignorant cannot understand the acts of a God, of a
Moses—or of a Wagner. What is frightening is the idea
that anyone, like a Moses, might have access to the totality
of knowledge because he will be capable of actions that are
beyond the capacities and comprehension of ordinary
human beings. We can have no defense against those who
know more. Even brute force would fail; but because this
is the one resort of the ignorant, the violence of the all-
knowing is fully justified. We are frightened by the idea
that anyone can have such great knowledge because we can
never predict what might be. Moses knows what to do,
because he knows the consequences of every possible action.*

*So if the paranoid personality is frightened by foreign voic-
es, Moses, on the contrary, uses those voices to frighten others. When I had postulated the existence of the superego as a
derivative of parental authority, and suggested that it was the
source of our conscience and sense of guilt, I was not
describing an all-knowing conscience. What I had overlooked
was that, as in the case of Moses, the superego can become
independent of the ego where it arose; should it do this it
will be described as frightening—"scary"—by the one who*

---

[3] This is interestingly prescient about the way today's cognitive
scientists talk. For example, I remember the first time the Marilyn
Machine squeaked out a vague imitation of Marilyn Monroe's
"Ooooooooh," Dicke looked at me and said, "Scary kid, real scary,
isn't it!" Thinking back on it now, I find Dicke more scary than our
machine. But maybe that's what he wanted me to think.

knows it (though he will surprisingly show no fear of it himself) because he knows all.

Of course, no human being can claim to have total knowledge and therefore that knowledge must come from somewhere else, if it exists at all. Hence Moses had to attribute his knowledge to information passed on to him by God. The source of this knowledge is then an hallucination and we should make a distinction between the superego postulated by psychoanalytic theory and what I will call this all-knowing superego, or hallucinatory superego.[4]

It is unlike ordinary hallucinations because it has a greater authority than any hallucination that the neurotic individual will ordinarily encounter. It is unrelated to the superego of psychoanalytic theory, which represents a special relationship between the individual and his parents and later social authorities; the hallucinatory superego represents a special relationship between the individual and the totality of knowledge.

Now we are in a better position to understand the nature of knowledge, belief and authority. Moses treated his followers with disdain and violence because they were incapable of having direct access to the knowledge that he had acquired. What is striking about Moses is that he is not awed or frightened by the knowledge to which he claims to have access. He talks to his hallucinatory super-

---

[4] The awe-inspiring, amoral *hallucinatory superego* reminds me of Jonathan Swift's *Gulliver* and Lewis Carroll's *Alice*. See Endnotes, pp. 169–170, for details.

ego as an equal. But it is also an essential characteristic of
Moses that he had to have followers. Without a group of
people who can be dominated by the knowledge a Moses
possesses, that knowledge is of no interest. We cannot go
further than this; future research will have to reveal the
conditions that are essential for creating an hallucinatory
superego.

In the history of religion new messiahs were forced to
change moral law to better stake their claims to originality.
Christ altered Moses' "Eye for an eye, a tooth for a tooth."
with "Turn the other cheek." And if Moses' God promised
"The land of milk and honey," Christ, a thousand years
later, said, "The poor shall inherit the earth." And of course,
when Moses reported that God would "bolt out of my
book" anyone who didn't listen to him and then God "sent
a plague upon the people," Christ said, "Love your enemies
and pray for those who persecute you."

Nonetheless, we do know that modern thinkers can no
longer use a God as a source of their global knowledge. In
the past there was always a glimmer of modesty in our
great men, because none had thought, even in their
moments of greatest folly, that they could have done it all
alone. They all needed help; they all needed to say God
had been there to help them.

But the extraordinary advance of knowledge, the mar-
velous achievements of this past century in spite of the dis-
asters of war, have changed the nature of our relation to
knowledge and the nature of our psyche. We know too

much to accept grandiose claims; indeed, we know so much that we know how little we know and that any explanation is going to be fraught with myriad new problems. We've become impatient with our knowledge, because we now need to know it all, and barring that, we at least want to claim that we have a glimpse of the whole, that we are beginning to get our bearings in a story that might be without limit, but that in our own lifetimes at least the essential outlines we have mastered.

The rise of modern science made the use of private evidence impossible. Consequently, what the modern "all-knowing" thinker does is to create a "theoretical" work that is so difficult that only he and his select group of associates (under his guidance) can understand it. The "theory" becomes a sacred text that must be revealed, interpreted during the following centuries. Since everything can be explained by the theory (it is total knowledge reduced to its most elementary form), its creator already knows every discovery that will be made in the future and hence will have no difficulty saying, when a new and unexpected discovery is made, "It's in the theory." Those who disagree will be treated with violence. Psychosis, not neurosis, is thus the key to our moral conscience.[5]

---

[5] As I have already noted, Freud's description of Wagner (and of megalomania in general) reminds me of Dicke in almost every detail. I often have the impression that Freud's discussion is indeed based on an intimate acquaintance with Norman Dicke, but I know that is impossible. It is odd because our relationships were quite different. Wagner and Freud were obviously comrades

I am not a moralist and I am in no way passing judgment on these men or the societies that hold them in such
esteem. If fraud is the basis of success, then so let it be.
Certainly our moral injunctions are important not because
they are meant to be followed, but on the contrary,
because they create great new pleasures by forbidding what
we most desire to do. These rules, these lists of "don'ts"
(often made by the very men who mean to disobey them),
create a new sense of pleasure.

I have argued in the past that the renunciation of pleasure that is forced upon us by the advances in civilization
will ultimately become intolerably "neurotic" and I now
must revise that view. While I have always recognized that
extreme suffering leads to modifications in individual psychology, I had failed to see that the sufferings of the neurotic can become the pleasures of the psychotic, that in
reaction to the restrictions and renunciations of pleasure
demanded by civilization, new and more dangerous pleasures would be found, that guilt (what I have argued is the
central problem of civilization because it forces upon us
renunciations of pleasure that become intolerable) can give
us new sources of pleasure, no doubt among them the

---

in their early years in research and though after that they each
went their separate ways intellectually, they maintained a friendly,
if distant, association throughout their lives. I, on the other hand,
knew Dicke only as a colleague. When I left him there was no
great intellectual divide between us, as there was between Wagner
and Freud. What divided us were those psychological needs of
Dicke that are the subject of the Freud *Manuscript*.

pleasure of transgression itself that drives the believer in the Ten Commandments to adultery and even murder. And so too how much more exciting for the would-be scientist, writer or artist to win acclaim for "global theories" that are far beyond anything actually achieved.

And thus it is that psychoanalysis, my creation, is doomed. I had always known this, but I had misunderstood why. I've always said that I, the discoverer of psychoanalysis, the first man to have analyzed himself—and being the first and only man who could know what the discovery of analysis is all about—am the ultimate judge of what is and what is not analysis. For there is a big difference between discovering and studying what has already been discovered.

Einstein's understanding of Relativity Theory is very different from that of everyone who came after him. No one can ever know what it was like for Einstein to have struggled with ideas that at the time seemed strange, if not downright absurd and wrong. It is the ability to confront what seems plainly wrong and then discover that it is right that is responsible for all intellectual and scientific advances.

The discovery of psychoanalysis was more difficult than most, if not all, scientific endeavors.[6] Einstein, after all, didn't invent physics, so he could ultimately be judged by other

[6] In Bernadette Schilder's copy of the *Manuscript* there is a discussion of the difference between psychological theory and other scientific theories that follows and that had been crossed out in red ink:

physicists. And he was. But analysis is something else alto-
gether. Nobody had ever tried to analyze himself before I
struggled with my own self-analysis. Nobody could possibly
know what it is like to come up with such bizarre, if not
repugnant, ideas as castration fears and penis envy, to strug-
gle against them, knowing that if you dared announce these
ideas in public you would be ridiculed for life. Einstein never
suffered ridicule.

And once you revealed the deep dark secrets that lurk in
all our minds, it would be impossible for anyone to make

Any psychological theory of worth would have to change
the way ordinary people think. People become guilty
because of their relations to each other, and guilt changes
the nature of those relations. What we say and think about
ourselves alters the way we understand others, and therefore
any theories we might have about human psychology are
meant to influence, as much as to describe, behavior.
Anyone who pretends he is giving a "scientific" description
of behavior does not understand the unrepeatable nature of
human behavior, nor what human psychology is all about.

Psychoanalytic theory would just not have been the same
if it had been one among many such theories and if it had
been presented as a hypothetical possibility. Psychoanalytic
theory has changed our notions of ourselves. Penis envy as
an abstract idea in some obscure academic journal was just
not the same thing as penis envy bantered about on trains,
in restaurants and in the public toilets. The nature of the
beast is something else altogether.

A psychological "theory" becomes a theory when it is
transformed by everyday usage, when it becomes part of the
fabric of everyday life. It is the every essence of any theory
about human psychology that it has to alter the way we
understand ourselves; human psychology cannot be simply
described.

the same discoveries and know and understand them the way you have. Even if my ideas had never won wide acceptance, future discoverers of castration fears knew what they were going to discover. They had been warned about the dangers of what they were doing. In fact, after I had successfully analyzed myself it became an unrepeatable act, a unique act of history, that could be studied, but that could only be imitated.

That was why it became important for me to train analysts. Patients needed guidance, or they would have come to the conclusions too quickly and failed to have understood what the process of self-discovery was all about. And, of course, the analysts, men and women whom I had trained, were themselves but shadows of myself. They too never could have known the truth about analysis. The very process of self-analysis makes hash of the idea of scientific verification. There are just certain things that cannot be repeated, and that doesn't make them any less true.

I have had to confront ridicule all my life; worse still, I have had to confront the revolt of my students, the men and women whom I taught, trained, and to whom I revealed hidden secrets that they never could have come upon themselves. I have had to reveal to them some of my deepest secrets, without, of course, compromising myself, or I never would have won their confidence in the first place.

In fact, it became evident to me that loyalty was not a quality that I could ever hope for among my followers. I knew that one day, each and every one of them would turn against me. I knew they would turn against me because

*they would resent that whatever secrets they discovered
with my assistance, and maybe even later on their own,
they would always know that they could never make the
real discovery of what it was all about, because they could
never repeat what I had done. The thrill of the original discovery would never be theirs—and the pain as well. It was
not even that I was unwilling to compromise myself. No
matter how much I did compromise myself—and in revealing secrets that were sure to lead to ridicule I had to and
did—still I could never reveal what it was like to make
these discoveries.*

*Self-discovery is one of our greatest desires. I had to destroy
all my letters—surely they would be misunderstood in the
future. Look as they may, the future nitpickers, scandalmon-
gers, would-be "scholars" can never know me; and they can
never know how my discoveries were made.*

*The only biography worthy of the name is hagiography,
as the writers of the Bible discovered long ago. The good
biography outlines events and leaves the reader to ponder
what greatness is all about. But those who would destroy
our reputations because of a letter found here, or a misplaced note left with a former admirer, leave the reader
totally uninformed. Certainly they can create scandal, certainly they can make a name for themselves on our reputations and save future generations from the "fraudulent"
science of those of us who created their world. Their ships
will float ever so briefly. We will remain afloat long after
they have tried their hand at destroying the past.*

Sadly, however, after me, all attempts at self-discovery or self-knowledge can never be complete. No matter how much I might attempt to tell you the details of my discovery, you would always be missing something about how I did it. Indeed, the very process of discovery makes it impossible for me to remember, to tell you all that happened to me. And the great weakness of analysis, which after me had to be guided by those whom I had trained, was that my students, like their students, would know that something was missing, something that I knew, that they could never know, was not there for them to discover. For they knew where their analysis was going, the castration fear and penis envy that would explain all at the end of their analyses.

I had robbed the future of the pleasure of self-discovery, which was unlike any other theft in history. Einstein may have robbed future physicists of the pleasure of discovering Relativity, but there is always more for future scientists to learn. Just as there is always more for us to learn, as I have always stressed, from analysis. But we all yearn after self-analysis, we all yearn to know ourselves as no one else can—for it is a fundamental law of psychology that we are self-reflective, self-conscious beings, and the most elementary form of our self-awareness is thinking about ourselves.

That would have been no longer possible if the discoveries of psychoanalysis had been all true. And that is why these discoveries were doomed from the beginning. They had built into them their own destruction, the guaranteed revolt of the followers, and the resistance of those who refused to recognize the accomplishments of analysis, because there would always be something about the very idea of self-analysis that could no longer be grasped. All were and are doing it because of me. They are analyzing themselves because of the explanations I had given about behavior; they are looking for the roots of their neuroses, seeking an explanation for some odd slip, because I had said these things could be explained and through these explanations a greater psychological freedom could be attained. But genuine self-analysis you have to do because of yourself, and once the idea becomes common coinage, that is no longer possible, and the whole enterprise, the whole science, is doomed. That was the paradox of the new science of analysis!

But then if psychoanalysis was doomed because it could never give the patient the ultimate insight that he was seeking into himself, it was doomed too because the very process of analysis takes too long. Wagner thought that he had an answer to lengthy analyses with his quick "cures." In fact, Wagner gave us a profound insight into the nature of "cure." If you could frighten sick patients into pretending that all is well, did it really matter that the "cure" was short-lived? Life itself is short. Little wonder the Nobel Committee was impressed with his Malaria Therapy.

But what Wagner really taught us was that he was the ultimate psychoanalyst. His cold indifference, surface veneer of concern, was what I had always insisted on for my students. Inflicting pain in the service of cure. And so too Moses and every megalomaniac who has inhabited the earth since. Analysis was doomed because only a megalomaniac could do it effectively; but a megalomaniac would not help the patient seek self-knowledge, but only submission.

And so what I came to understand was that the problem of civilization was not a sense of guilt, the remorse for some primal crime, the killing of the "father," but the mentality of the "father," whose arbitrary rules and explanations, whose brutality in the name of those rules, had psychological roots that bore no resemblance to anything I had discussed during more than a quarter of a century of careful study and analysis of patients and myself. In trying to discover a science of the mind, I discovered the extraordinary complexity of the very questions that we must ask ourselves and attempt to answer in order to create such a science. Of course, it is fortunate that we never come up with all the answers—in truth we never come even close to knowing the springs of our thoughts and actions—so that we are not only giving free reign to future generations, but plenty to scorn in our pretensions to having explained so much.

"The Tower of Babel"
(An unfinished essay found on Freud's desk at the time of his death.)

[Shortly after Bernadette Schilder and I approached the committee of the Freud Archives with the *Megalomania* manuscript, they released this essay for publication with the *Manuscript*. The Archives requested that the following notice be included with the publication:

"The mission of the Freud Archives has been to protect the reputations of Freud's family, friends, acquaintances and patients, as well as their immediate descendants, and that mission would have been frequently compromised if the Archives had commented on the numerous scholarly discussions since the death of Sigmund Freud that have raised questions about Freud's motivations and personal life. As Freud's heritage is, we believe, one of science and philosophy, we have always tried to provide whatever materials might be relevant for discussions within the scientific and intellectual community and the Archives have, therefore, from time to time, released letters and other documents that might be useful to these ends.

"The Committee has, we must confess, always

been rather puzzled by Freud's final notes, written a few days before he died. We have on several occasions in the past been tempted to release this document to the general and scholarly public, but as its theoretical importance was unclear we have, perhaps erringly, thought it better that the document remain sealed until the date Freud himself had proposed his letters and unpublished works be released—2039. As the document makes reference to several persons whose descendants are still living, and as its purpose was unclear, we have had to stand by this decision over the years.

"The recent discovery of the *Megalomania* manuscript, whose authenticity the Committee does not doubt, though the reasons for our conviction must remain, for the moment, sealed, as family members would indeed be compromised if the relevant documents in the Archives were released, has shed an entirely new light on the document the Archives is releasing today. It is now apparent that the document in question was written as an appendage to the *Manuscript* and it sheds new light not only on that work, but Freud's entire opus. Indeed, we believe that it tells us much about a famous, if not important, episode in modern history and, as Freud has proved with his well-known works, demonstrates a foresight concerning the development of the modern science, that the present epoch cannot ignore. The Committee has therefore unanimously decided to release the document in the Archives to which Freud had given the provisional title 'The Tower of Babel.' "

The manuscript was translated by Bernadette Schilder.

—A.J.S.]

---

5 September 1939

*M*y daughter Anna was embarrassed to tell me this morning that a stranger had called on several occasions this past week asking to see me and that she had, given my condition, told him that I was not even seeing close friends. But when he returned this morning with a document I will presently discuss, Anna asked the man to come by this afternoon and said that if I should consent she would permit him to see me for half an hour. He left the document behind and when she showed it to me, I did not hesitate to accept to see the unknown visitor. My daughter has always had an uncommon sense of what might bring me great pleasure and I must use whatever forces I can muster to record, in however sketchy a fashion, the visit of this most uncommon man.

As Anna had told me nothing about him, having merely shown me the document that I have already mentioned, I was surprised when a man of my own age, fluent in German, was ushered into my study in the midafternoon.

*He introduced himself as Maurice Koechlin and apolo-
gized for his slight hesitation in German, because he had,
he explained, rarely used the language since his studies in
Zurich in the last quarter of the past century. He explained
to me he was born in Alsace the same year I was born in
Moravia, and had fled his hometown when the Germans
had invaded in 1871 and become a Swiss citizen during his
studies in Zurich.*

*He was an odd mixture of modesty and self-assurance,
his modesty perhaps suggested by his slight linguistic dis-
comfort. He had studied at the Polytechnicum, where he
had been the top student; he had then gone to Paris to
work for the Compagnie des Chemins de Fer de l'Est and
subsequently the Société des Etablissements Eiffel. There
he was responsible for making all the important calculations
for a number of important architectural structures in
Europe and the United States.*

*Despite my familiarity with some of the projects that he
mentioned to me, I had to confess that I had never heard
his name. Koechlin smiled timidly when I said this to him
and excused himself for perhaps tiring me. But I was hardly impatient with his story and I told him to continue,
since I wanted to understand how the document that Anna
had shown me the previous day, and which was now lying
on my desk, had come into being.*

*Again he apologized unnecessarily and told me that
there had been much talk in architectural and engineering
circles in the last quarter of the century about the difficul-*

ties the Americans had encountered in the building of the
monumental obelisk in Washington. They had hardly
reached some sixty meters when they had discovered that it
was beginning to lean and it was only years later that the
work was resumed and a somewhat shorter edifice was
completed.

In 1876, for the anniversary of the American Revolution,
two Americans, Clark and Reeves, had written a proposal in
which they had said that they wanted to "imitate the first
descendants of Noah" who had sought to immortalize
themselves in an enormous tower of brick and mortar and
that therefore they thought it would be appropriate for the
youngest of the world's nations to celebrate its centennial
with its own Tower of Babel, as they called it, a one-thou-
sand-foot iron column that would put into relief by its con-
trast with the world's oldest architectural ambitions, the
striking transformations of science and the arts through the
ages. But the project never saw the light of day.

What was extraordinary about the American project,
Koechlin said, was that it avoided the pitfalls of the
Washington obelisk and indeed a tower much higher than
one thousand feet would have been possible. The
American project was reported in France in the magazine
La Nature and was widely discussed in architectural and
engineering circles.

And then in May of 1884, architects became excited
about the coming Universal Exhibition in Paris that was to
celebrate the centennial of the French Revolution. Koechlin

and an associate in his office, Émile Nouguier, wondered between themselves what might give the Exhibition a particular allure and had, no doubt inspired by the Americans, the idea of building an enormous iron tower. It was the evening of the 6th of June that Koechlin made some preliminary calculations and produced the document that was lying on my desk, a drawing that bore an unmistakable resemblance to one of the most famous architectural achievements of recent times, the Eiffel Tower.

Koechlin held the drawing in his hands for several minutes and then, replacing it on the desk in front of me, said that it was with certain relief and yet deep disappointment that he and his colleague had reacted when they showed their project to the head of the company, Gustave Eiffel. When I asked him what he meant, he said that it was only recently that he recalled his sense of excitement when Eiffel told them that he was in no way interested in their project, but saw no reason why they shouldn't pursue their idea.

He had been working for Eiffel for five years and had been responsible for making all the important calculations, as he had already told me, for the bridges that had brought Eiffel considerable fame in the engineering and architectural world and, of course, he added, almost as an afterthought, he had calculated and designed the interior of Bartholdi's Statue of Liberty that the public believed had been the work of Gustave Eiffel. He was pleased that Eiffel had categorically rejected their projected tower, because he believed it would be his first opportunity to construct an important monument in his own name.

He and Nouguier persisted, seeking the assistance of the firm's principal architect, Stephen Sauvestre, who reworked Koechlin's original drawing. Sauvestre added the "decorations" that made the project more grandiose and aesthetic, including the lacework that joined the four feet of the tower and a large glass-enclosed space on the first landing. It was this drawing that they showed to Bartholdi, who subsequently exhibited the plans. When they showed Eiffel their new version of the tower he found the idea of such great interest that on September 18th, 1884, he took out a patent on the work in his name and that of Nouguier and Koechlin.

Eiffel's enthusiasm now knew no bounds. They had no sooner received the patent than Eiffel invited Koechlin, Nouguier and Sauvestre to dinner and, suggesting that he could better exploit their idea himself, offered to buy the exclusive rights to the patent, both in France and the rest of the world. And he would pay each of them one percent of any fees he might receive for the building of the tower. Of course, Koechlin added uncertainly, he promised that he would give them full credit if the tower was built.

It was then that Koechlin paused in his narrative and looked at me. He again suggested that he was tiring me and that it might be best that he leave. But to reassure him I told him that though we were the same age and I was certainly in poorer health, he had come to me with a story that was a perfect example of a matter that had lately been preoccupying me. He appeared confused by my remark, but I encouraged him to continue.

He said, what he might have thought had been in my

mind, that he and his colleagues realized "a pittance" compared with what Eiffel eventually earned from the exploita-
tion of the patent. But it wasn't what I had been thinking.
What I wanted to know was how the tower had been built.

He was embarrassed by my question. Surely he had been
asked the same question on many occasions, and he had
found his own explanations wanting. No doubt, when he
had filled in the details that he was about to tell me, others
had said to him, "So what?," convincing him that the
implicit claims he was making to me were not justified by
his own accounting. But he was wrong about my interest
and my tentative conclusions.

The man I was listening to was typical of many patients
I had seen during my career. He was a man overwrought
by his own doubts, who nonetheless felt that he had not
received his due. And he had come to me, not out of any
hope that I would tell him that life had been unfair to him,
but, as I had so often seen in my neurotic patients, because
of those very doubts, his inability to resolve a conflict that,
when he tried to reason it out with himself, or his friends
and colleagues, seemed perfectly straightforward. And yet
no matter how much conviction he brought to his own
analyses, he remained crippled by something he could not
understand.

What Koechlin did not know was that it was my understanding of the nature of that very conflict that was now
undergoing a profound change in my own mind. I was fortunate that Koechlin was not versed in psychoanalytic literature.

If I had been a superstitious man I would have said fate had sent him to me; but I knew his visit was but a lucky accident, which if I had more time and strength, I would have wanted to investigate in greater depth than is now possible for me.

My students and colleagues would be very surprised that a man who was in every way my contemporary would have intrigued me in ways that none of them could have understood or suspected. I was glad to avoid the obvious, glad that Koechlin was ignorant of my work, and was annoyed when Anna poked her head in the door, hinting that Koechlin might be tiring me. I reassured her that I was fine—and indeed, I had forgotten about my condition—and as she quietly closed the door I asked Koechlin to continue with his tale. I was unusually moved by him and this was something that I could not remember having felt for a patient in a very long time. He was a man who appeared to know his own worth, a man who knew that he had been capable of major achievements and indeed had fulfilled those capabilities, and yet who had deep nagging doubts about his worth. He spoke about Eiffel with neither great admiration nor any sign of bitterness. Yet Eiffel occupied a considerable place in his mental life.

When I repeated my question, how the tower had been built, Koechlin, somewhat puzzled, said that Eiffel had written a three-volume Biographie *in the third person. " 'This tower is Monsieur Eiffel's magnum opus,' " Koechlin recited by heart from Gustave Eiffel's book, " 'and is a symbol of strength and difficulties overcome.' "*

*And in his third-person autobiography Eiffel dated the
conception of the tower from 1886, when in fact, as we
know, the original design was made in 1884. He once
again took the drawing from my desk and with a terribly
puzzled look told me that it had been on exhibit at the
recent World's Fair in Paris but had not drawn any comment from the press or, as far as he knew, the general public. I was charmed by his belief that documentary evidence
would have altered what was clearly part of contemporary
mythology. I told him that the generally held beliefs of
societies are the consequence of our ignorance of where
our societies are going, our inability to know what will
happen from one day to the next and our attempts to
cover up, to cajole and fool ourselves, that we might have
some sense of coherence in our lives. For ultimately, an
understanding of ourselves requires an understanding of
what will happen tomorrow and the day after tomorrow
and our mental stability depends on our belief that our
judgments are correct. We convince ourselves, should we
happen to have guessed right that we do understand ourselves, that we are in control of our destinies, though we
know, if we bother to reflect upon it, that this is truly
impossible. It is our day-to-day destiny that we seek to
control and with this control establish a psychological
equilibrium without which our daily lives would fall apart.
To question the authorship of the Eiffel Tower—an object
of neither utility nor importance, but an object and a name
that nonetheless are part of established truths whose very
simplicity and irrelevancy form part of the backbone of our*

willingness to accept other much more important "truths"
about ourselves and our relations to others—is to destroy
our confidence in our understanding of the social fabric on
which our ever-so-frail psychological equilibrium depends.
Little wonder the public looked at, and ignored,
Koechlin's original drawing of the tower.[1]

[1] Freud's view of Koechlin is largely supported by the latter's *Journal.* Koechlin kept a diary of his visits to Freud. As can be seen in the following entry that the family has kindly allowed me to print, Koechlin's comments confirm Freud's suspicions. In fact, as the Freud scholar Kurt Fischer has kindly informed me, Freud had encountered similar ambivalence among his own followers either whenever he made important revisions in his theory, or when he incorporated other's ideas into his own works without giving any credit. In the *Manuscript* Freud is not condoning such behavior; rather, without passing moral judgment—such judgments would be irrelevant and misleading—he argues that this kind of behavior is fundamental to social stability. Documentary evidence that destroys long-accepted "truths" must be ignored. Societies develop a kind of blindness to whatever might disturb the social order. And certainly this is the point of Freud's comments, later in his essay, about the moral indignation of the Eiffels and the Wagners when accused of wrongdoing. An individual's worth, his psychological stability, depends not on the "truths" concerning his past, but on the social acceptance of those truths. Freud seems to be suggesting that if society "assigned" the works of a Freud or an Einstein to any ordinary citizen and treated him with all the honors due the historical Freud or Einstein, the ordinary man would have no psychological difficulty accepting his assigned role—indeed he would become so comfortable with it that any challenge to his authority would be treated with disdain.

It was this phenomenon that is central to the argument of the *Manuscript* that Koechlin was unable to grasp, and that was certainly at the heart of the public's blindness when confronted by the original drawing of the tower at the Universal Exhibition in

*I didn't insist on this. Anna once again knocked on the
door and said that it was unwise for me to continue the
interview but, seeing my disappointment, suggested that
Mr. Koechlin might be able to come back the following day.*

*Koechlin returned the following afternoon at the
appointed hour. He was unusually agitated and said he had
many things to tell me, having spent the night thinking
about our conversation of the previous day. True enough,
he said, once Eiffel had bought the rights to the tower he
began an enormous publicity campaign, publishing numerous pamphlets describing "his" tower. He was able to win
the support of the important members of the Universal
Exhibition committee and when an international competition was announced, architects were given a mere two
weeks to submit plans for a tower that the committee said
would be one of the main attractions of the exhibit. Eiffel*

Paris in 1937. Indeed, Koechlin's story was once again presented
to the general public at the time of the centennial of the Eiffel
Tower (1989) in numerous publications that were presumably
widely read. But even the authors of these books recounted the
story as Koechlin had told it to Freud and yet none called their
book *Koechlin's Tower*, or felt compelled to praise Eiffel's associates as much as they praised Eiffel himself. It is hardly surprising
that the full force of their words was lost on the reading public,
since the authors themselves were unable to accept the true significance of their own arguments. (See, for example, Bernard
Lemoine, *La Tour de Monsieur Eiffel*, Paris: La Découverte
[Gallimard], 1989: "*son génie* [de Eiffel] *n'est pas d'avoir inventé
la Tour, c'est de l'avoir réalisée et de lui avoir donné son nom*" [p.
29]. Eiffel's genius was not to have invented the tower, but to
have to have produced it and to have given it his name.) None of
this would have surprised the author of the *Manuscript*.

*won the competition in spite of considerable resistance to
his plans.*

*Of course, Koechlin said with a confidence he seemed to
have acquired during his reflections the previous evening,
Eiffel Enterprises had considerable experience in building
some of the most daring bridges in Europe, and he,*

Here is the entry in Koechlin's *Journal*:
It was certainly a mistake for me to release the drawing of
the tower at such a late date, but it is impossible for me to
convince people that it would have served no purpose at the
time. I thought Freud, who has a reputation as great as
Gustave Eiffel's, could have told me what was wrong with
my attempt to present *documentary* evidence to the public
about the Tower. I was not trying to take any credit from
Eiffel, as Freud seemed to believe. I was merely trying to
note, for the record, that we—Nouguier, Sauvestre and I—
were very much a part of the project and that without us it
probably never would have come into being. Freud kept
insisting that I was wrong and I couldn't convince him that
I, after all, should know, since I had been present at all the
events I was describing to him. He told me that I was
deceiving myself about my own importance and said that
there was nothing he could do about "self-deception." He
said that I must have been terribly pleased when Eiffel went
on trial and was convicted for the Panama affair [see pp.
149–150]. But this just wasn't true. I was very upset by the
public humiliation Gustave suffered in those years and felt
personally humiliated too, though I had nothing to do with
his Panama dealings. In fact, it was following the Panama
affair that I lost any desire to set the record straight about
the Tower. I had never wanted to humiliate Eiffel and I am
sure that the press would have sought to dramatize what
was simply a matter of record. Probably the only joy Eiffel
had in the years following the "affair" was the construction
of the Tower and I think his suffering had been so great
that I was glad that he could at least enjoy recalling the

Koechlin, he said proudly, once again repeating what he had already told me, had been responsible for all the calculations and the on-site overseeing of all these constructions. And like the bridges, the tower had been completely prefabricated; every beam had been carefully measured and cut in the factory and all the rivet holes had been drilled before they were delivered to the construction site. If there had been an error of as much as a centimeter in the holes, the beams could not have been fitted and the tower would have taken many years to construct. Koechlin had personally made more than 1,700 of the general drawings and had supervised in his office the more detailed 3,629 drawings that were used by Émile Nouguier to cut the beams.

------

years we had spent in its construction without having to confront further humiliation because I showed the original design to the press. What I hoped Freud would have explained was why, when there was no longer any danger of adding to Eiffel's troubles, and the original drawing was exhibited, it went entirely unnoticed. I didn't understand what Freud meant when he said that I was asking too much because more than the Tower was at stake. By calling the authorship of the Tower into question (which is not what I was really doing) I was challenging deeply rooted beliefs about society. Honestly, I had no idea what he was talking about and I decided that it served no further purpose troubling a man who was obviously in very frail health. Psychology is really not much of a science!

Nonetheless, Koechlin added a long wavy line, a question mark, an exclamation mark and then in an unsteady hand, "Maybe I was duped!"

And Eiffel, I asked him—what did Eiffel have to do with the construction?

He looked at me, puzzled, and said, "Well, it was his tower. He had made it possible, had gotten all the financing. It was his."

He said this with a self-assurance that I imagined he must have shown almost half a century ago, when in the excitement of the construction and the enormous publicity it had attracted he certainly would have said exactly what he was telling me.

He was startled when I asked him if he believed that it was really Eiffel's tower. Certainly that was why he had come to me, but sitting in my office he hesitated and, stumbling over his words, said that, well, yes, it was Eiffel's tower, he had never said otherwise. He had always worked for Eiffel and he had never believed that Eiffel hadn't been responsible for the success of all the projects he had worked on. He owed everything to Eiffel, he had never denied that.

So why had he come to me? Why had he shown me the drawing? I asked him, and he looked at me as if he were puzzled by my questions. For a moment he sat there paralyzed. I had seen all this before, the conflict with oneself, what I had always argued stemmed from a guilt arising in childhood conflicts. But it wasn't guilt that had made millions of visitors to the recent World's Fair in Paris ignore, or view with indifferent curiosity, Koechlin's original design for the tower. Probably not one among them had

noticed the incongruity, the false history of the monument
that had become a symbol of their country.[2] The challenge
to authority is certainly not moral, and our acceptance of it
depends on a psychology that derives not from an ambivalence, a sense of guilt, as I have formerly argued, but on a
need for psychological stability, a need for a framework
within which we can organize our daily activities.

If we don't challenge authority, it is because we have
nothing to replace it with; we have no hope of ourselves
taking over and, worse still, if we lose those who are shap-
ing our lives, we will find ourselves at sea, unable to organize our own lives that social structures have organized for
us. That was Koechlin's problem. He owed everything to
Eiffel and to have claimed greater credit—as he no doubt
should have done—would have destroyed the very fabric
of social relations that had brought him whatever success
he had. He knew he needed Eiffel; and he also knew that
as long as he was dependent on him he could not satisfy
his own needs and desires.

Morality is clearly irrelevant to our social structures and
our mental stability. It is our paralysis, not our guilt, that

---

[2] Freud was probably not aware of another aspect of the "false
history" of the Eiffel Tower. Sophie Germain (1776–1831) was a
brilliant mathematician whose work on the mathematical theory of
elasticity was crucial in the construction of the tower. Her name is
not to be found on the inscription on the tower of seventy-two
names of individuals whose work contributed to its construction.
(See E. T. Bell, *Men of Mathematics*, New York: Simon & Schuster
[Firestone Books], 1965, pp. 261–263; and Simon Singh, *Fermat's
Last Theorem*, London: The Fourth Estate, 1997, p. 119.)

characterizes our relation to authority; and it is that very
paralysis that is the only moral and psychological challenge
we can pose to those who have stolen what we rightly consider our own. Indeed, given the opportunity, as Koechlin
was about to tell me he had, we become paralyzed by our
own "moral" strictures. We cannot claim for ourselves what
is rightly ours, because to make these claims convincing we
must do to others what was once done to us; it is not our
fear of doing wrong that paralyzes us, but our fear that in
doing wrong we might not succeed. What we call "morality" is ultimately fear, fear of failure where others have
allowed us at least a modicum of psychological calm; morality is fear and condemns us to a psychological ambivalence
from which there is no issue.

Indeed, Koechlin, though he was unable to say so in as
many words, had his opportunity. When I asked him what
he did about Eiffel's theft of his work, he didn't answer me
directly. He suddenly became very confident and said that
it wasn't necessary to do anything. The tower was still
under construction when Eiffel began negotiating another
spectacular contract to build the Panama Canal at what
would prove to be great profit to himself.

In the early 1890s, when the tower was still one of the
most popular attractions in the world, the company
responsible for the financing of the canal became bankrupt
and it emerged that there had been fraudulent manipulations on the part of the principal financiers, the Lesseps.
Many small investors lost their savings in the scandal and
the Lesseps and Eiffel were condemned to prison.

Koechlin told the story with considerable pride. On appeal Eiffel's prison sentence was quashed; he had not participated in the financial operations of the company but had been simply a contractor hired by the financiers. He was allowed to keep the millions of francs that he had reaped as profit, but his image was tarnished.

Koechlin must have seen this as his revenge. Yet his own failure became evident when Eiffel left him in charge of the construction company; while it remained a successful commercial operation under his aegis, it never again was in the public spotlight. Indeed, Koechlin was never able to use his position to claim the credit that had driven him to talk to me forty years after the events.

But Koechlin was also an emissary from my past, from a time when with great confidence I would have offered him a path to self-discovery that could have resolved the conflicts that were so much a part of his story. But now I had lost faith in my own views, and when Koechlin left that afternoon he must have been disappointed in me. I never saw him again.

There is something more to this story that I wish I could fully grasp. I still do not understand the Eiffels of the world, men who without the slightest hint of regret accept the accolades of friends, colleagues and the public in general, for work that they must know is not their own. The hollowness of their success suggests that my investigations into my own and my patients' pasts was a false path leading nowhere.

It seems that what we do and what we have done is of no importance. It is all a charade in search of glory at any price. Our worth is not our own, not that of our lives and works, but the worth a society puts on us. What troubles us is not ourselves; what we want, need and seek is the admiration of others, and admiration, even for false qualities, is an end in itself. If we are social animals, our societies, our families, our friends, mean only so much to us as the values they place upon us.[3]

The conflicts that I had once believed to be integral to our psyches are an internalization of an external drive for recognition. That we are prepared to accept the approval and admiration of others at any cost is a reflection of the complexity of modern societies, the compulsion to make our place within those societies noticed. Indeed, having won social approval, we cannot understand any challenge to what we believe to be our moral authority; there is no distinction, in the minds of the Eiffels and the Wagners and the Kozlowskis, between authority and "moral" authority, and the failure to make any distinction is an

---

[3] Freud's discussion here, though it is not directly concerned with the subject of money, suggests that the invention of money was driven by deep psychological needs that go well beyond the usual claims that link it to power. Perhaps even more important is that money allows an individual to claim credit, to have prestige without anyone asking *why* or *how* he came to acquire such status. It may be Freud fails to discuss the issue because he had argued that money is "filth," "dirt," "excrement," etc., in his earlier works, ideas that already imply that the genius of money is that the past (how we got it) is irrelevant.

inherent characteristic of our psychology. *A society that has held a Gustave Eiffel in such great esteem cannot reverse itself and accuse him of wrongdoing, because there is nothing a man in authority can do that is wrong; hence Eiffel's taking umbrage at the accusations against him in the Panama affair and hence too Wagner's taking umbrage at the accusations against him following the Great War. Those without authority, the weak, raise "moral" challenges against those in authority, but the reason is not moral superiority, but a psychological need to be noticed. What we call morality is the individual psyche's attempt to assert its importance, to give the individual a feeling of importance. And it is of no consequence if we win our claim to being recognized through fraud, cunning, murder and violence or through truly superior abilities. What we need is recognition; how we get it is of no concern to our psyche. It is not with our past that we must come to terms, but how we can successfully dupe others in rewriting that past to our own glory.* We are not obsessed by memories, but by the invention of memories that will work to our own advantage.

If I had once believed that self-discovery was a sufficient end in itself, I now must admit that I have deluded myself and all those who believed what I have so confidently taught. We exist in relation to others and at the heart of the complex nexus of forces that attract and repel us to and from each other is the need to know that others cannot ignore our existence. Petty thievery is, no doubt, the poor man's attempt to prove his importance in society; and tyranny, intellectual and political, might well be the ulti-mate and only meaningful satisfaction men can accept as the source of their own sense of worth. We follow our leaders out of a desire to be like them ourselves and like the Koechlins we remain with them, admire them, because they have proved themselves capable of fooling so many people so much of the time. I wonder if I too might not admire a man who could convince the world that he, not I, is the author of the works I have slaved over for a lifetime.[4]

---

[4] Perhaps the last complete sentence Freud wrote during his lifetime. It is followed by several sentences that have been crossed out and cannot be deciphered. Freud is probably referring here to Emma Benesch-Schilder and the *Manuscript* he left with her mother, Adelaide Benesch. This is suggested by some odd jottings at the bottom of the same page: "Emma" and "Emma B.; Emma B-F." Freud's concern with authorship, when his published works and his name were by now well-known—indeed he was among the most famous men of his day, if not of his century—must stem from his doubts about the uses to which Emma or some future grandchild he would never know might have put his manuscript. Or was his deeper concern with his own reputation—could Freud (in challenging Freud) leave behind a work that would surpass his own best efforts and forever alter his legacy?

ANNA FREUD:
Notes on a Conversation with
Johnny von Neumann

[When the Freud Archives learned of the *Megalomania* manuscript, they released "The Tower of Babel" essay presented on the previous pages. Shortly before the *Manuscript* went to press, I also received from the Committee Anna Freud's notes on a conversation she had had with John von Neumann in London sometime in the early 1950s. The manuscript is not dated, but the Freud Archives suggested it was probably written during the summer of 1980. During their afternoon tea, von Neumann spoke of the relation between the Freudian theory and the theories that were beginning to emerge from the newly developing fields of cybernetics and the computer sciences, today's cognitive sciences. I have briefly commented on this in my Introduction. I am grateful to the Archives for sending me these notes and giving me permission to publish them with the Freud manuscript. Only some minor alterations in punctuation have been made. The notes were written in English and were probably not meant for publication. But because of the light they might shed on the present work, I feel that Anna Freud would have approved of their publication as a conclusion to her father's last major work. I hope the reader will agree with my judgment.

—A.J.S.]

———◦◦◦———

An article in this morning's *Times* about a chess-playing computer reminded me of Johnny von Neumann's last visit to Hampstead more than twenty years ago.[1] I had known Johnny as a young mathematical genius who taught in Germany. He later helped the Americans build the bomb; after the war he had wanted to build bigger bombs and drop them on the Russians. But I had never imagined that the little book his wife Klara sent to me after his death—Johnny's posthumous *The Computer and the Brain*—would have helped launch a radical new view of human nature.

His cousin Ferenczi had sent us Johnny's paper on Game Theory in 1928 and had insisted that it was very profound and that it would one day prove to be

[1] I have been unable to find the article that Anna Freud is referring to. The *Times* has no general index for the years 1979 and 1980, when it is assumed Anna Freud wrote this memoir.

very important for our understanding of how we deal
with each other from day to day.[2] But the depth of
Johnny's paper escaped us and when Johnny came to
Vienna years later, he and my father spent the afternoon playing poker and telling each other jokes. He
was a terrible bluffer and a very sore loser, but my
father didn't seem to mind. It's a pity that at the time
Johnny hadn't as yet understood the connection
between his work and my father's. I'm sure my father
would have been fascinated.

That afternoon when I saw him alone in Hampstead
he *did* see the connection. It wasn't obvious at first
when he talked about his machines and how they
would imitate everything that went on in the human
brain; nor was it obvious when he said that he looked
forward to the day when he could build a machine that
had perfected the arts of bluffing and double-dealing.
But then he said he had been reading Freud recently
and he had concluded that Freud had believed (as did
Johnny) that the understanding of deception and distrust was critical to our understanding of *all* forms of
human behavior and *how the mind works*. And with a
bravado that I must confess left me speechless he told

---

[2] See Endnote 6 on pp. 165–166 for details about von
Neumann and his 1928 paper. Sándor Ferenczi (1873–1933) was
one of Freud's closest associates. He and von Neumann were
from Budapest and were indeed cousins.

me that Freud's theory of the unconscious, repression and Oedipus was, if you really studied it carefully, about self-deception, double-dealing and reprisals.

"Right?"

I wasn't sure. And yet there was something in what he had said that continued to trouble me long after he was gone.

I never saw him again.

I thought it was odd that a man who so loved to bluff should have believed that there was a *logic* to deception that you could put into a machine, or that the art of winning was merely a long series of calculations. It was odd because Johnny von Neumann *enjoyed* deception for deception's sake. I remember his insisting that chess just isn't a real game. Once you knew what it was all about, you could be assured of winning (or losing, if you started on the wrong side). It was *not knowing* how your bluffing would turn out that really excited him. If Johnny had won every single encounter—if he had known in advance that he would always win—winning just wouldn't have been any fun for him—or any one else, for that matter. Of course, he got very upset when he lost, when pranks were played on him; but it was the uncertainty, the suspense, that made the bluff, the lie, worth the while. And yet Johnny insisted on discovering the underlying rationality to uncertainty—he wanted to live in a world of suspense, but he wanted to be able to predict the outcome. I remember his admitting that there was something wrong with his "theory."[3]

So I was troubled when he told me that Freudian theory, a theory I had watched evolve from day to day, was about something that had never come to my mind before—that *repression* was just another way of talking about an *expert strategist*, a *bluffer*, a *liar* and a *deceiver*. (If there was a difference between Freud and von Neumann it was that Johnny was more interested in how we bluff and deceive *each other*, while Freud wanted to know about how we deceive *ourselves*.)[4] Freud,

---

[3] Anna Freud's discussion here implies that a man who tells lies without thinking of himself as a liar "thinks" like a machine. He is not aware of himself. Lying requires an ability to think about oneself. If a machine "claims" to be Greta Garbo, there's not much point in accusing it of lying, since, in fact, machines can't really "talk" about themselves. The problem with the pathological liar—who may, in some sense, lack self-awareness—is that telling him he is a liar (that is, telling him that he is not what he claims to be) is denying that he exists.

[4] Readers of Freud's *Manuscript* will find themselves less puzzled by von Neumann's claims than Anna Freud was, since we know that in the *Manuscript* Freud himself thought of self-deception as a central feature of the psyche and even suggested that this had always been one of his principal ideas. Indeed, the *Manuscript*, we might argue, "rescues" the Freudian *oeuvre* with this new view and thereby establishes a very deep link with the central problems raised by von Neumann. Both Freud and von Neumann considered an understanding of the mechanisms of *deception* essential for revealing the nature of the psyche, though each approached the question from quite different points of view. The contemporary cognitive sciences have yet to recognize the importance of this question. Perhaps this will change because of the *Manuscript*.

Johnny said, was becoming part of a very sophisticated mathematical science. I guess I should have been happy for my father, but at the time I was rather puzzled.[5]

And yet all that talk about bluffing and deception reminded me of something very odd that happened one night when I had come in late. My father's light was on and I had knocked lightly on his door and opened it without waiting for a response. I thought he might have fallen asleep and was rather surprised to see him busily writing at his desk. He too was surprised. He looked up at me without saying a word, holding his pen in midair, a pained look on his face. I stood there and asked him if he'd like some tea. But he said he was in the middle of something; he feared

---

[5] Some readers, familiar with the contemporary arguments that Freud was no scientist, "quite lacking in the empirical and ethical scruples that we would hope to find in any responsible scientist, to say nothing of a major one," (see Frederick Crews, *The Memory Wars, op. cit.*) might be astonished to learn that John von Neumann, whose scientific credentials are impeccable by any standards, would have spoken of computer simulations as more "rigorous" extensions of Freud's work. Freud's famous statement that "an instinct never becomes the object of consciousness—only the idea that represents the instinct can" ("The Unconscious" in SE 14:177) is not very different from the contemporary cognitive scientist's that "we are not aware of the computations, the physical manipulations of symbols, but only of the *ideas* those symbols represent; in the same way we are not aware of the state of the computer circuitry but only the words and images we see on the computer screen because of circuitry." For Norbert Weiner's comments on Game Theory, see the Endnotes, p. 170.

he'd "lose" it if he stopped just then. And he said "Good night" while gesturing that I close the door.

I had never been dismissed by him like that before and I wanted to believe that it was because of his illness. Yet, no matter how much I tried to convince myself, the truth of the matter was, I *knew* he was doing something at that moment that he didn't want me to see. *He was writing something he didn't want me to see.* I was convinced, because I searched his study the next day for the papers I had seen piled neatly on his desk. The sheet he had been writing upon when I walked in had the name and address of the Hotel Brésil in Paris printed on the top. He had been writing on the reverse side of the paper; the side facing me was blank. The organization of the papers on his desk suggested that he was working on a manuscript. But why had he chosen to write a manuscript on some old hotel stationery? And why had my discovering him in the act of writing so upset him?

He spent the next two days in his study and I decided not to disturb him. Jones came around with two students and Freud spoke to them for an hour. He told them not to take Oedipus too seriously, by which he meant, he said, that we are really fragmentary selves, sliding from one personality into another, desperately trying to fit into the world. We pull ourselves together with our obsessions that give us the illusion of being "one," "ourselves," allowing us to ignore, rather than adapt to, those around us. He said he had observed long ago that obsessional ideas are disguised in a remarkable verbal vagueness that allowed them to be used in many different circumstances. He was looking at me, not at Jones or his students. I know he was talking about those pages he had been writing on the back of the hotel stationery.

I'm sure he was still working on that manuscript a week later when I knocked on his study and I could hear the shuffling of papers before he told me to come in. And I'm almost certain he was carrying "it" with him that afternoon in Paris when he left us for a few hours and he returned empty-handed. I don't know if he thought I suspected anything when I had walked in on him that night. I never asked him and he never spoke about it. There were times when he appeared terribly uncomfortable in my presence, when he must have feared I was about to ask him what he had been writing. He had a way of looking at me and forbidding me to speak. But I never did ask him. Maybe I was being a good poker player.

Johnny had said, "Good poker players know there are moments when you don't call the other players' bluff. You don't want them to know just how clever you are."

He had added, "And then there are moments when you must call the other player's bluff."

I never called Freud's bluff, but I never saw his hand either. I'm not sure I ever wanted to know what my father was writing that night. Poker players may enjoy the bluff, but there are forms of deception that are just too painful for us to want to know about. That's what my father was really talking about when he spoke of repression and maybe that night he put me to the test.

"Regrettably," Johnny said before leaving that afternoon, "we don't have a 'theory' of deception, but only an imperfectly articulated and hardly formalized 'body of experience.'"

It's more than forty years since father died and still there's no sign of that manuscript. I sometimes wonder if the whole thing isn't an invention of my imagination, if what I 'remember' seeing never happened.[6]

---

[6] As I have noted in my Introduction, the *Megalomania* manuscript was written on the reverse side of writing paper from the Hotel Brésil in Paris. Anna Freud's recollection is undoubtedly accurate. It is impossible to know what she might have thought and what suspicions might or might not have been confirmed had she lived to see the publication of the *Manuscript*. She might have been dismayed to learn of the existence of her younger half-sister. Still, it is remarkable that it was the recollection of von Neumann's visit that appears to have reawakened her interest in her father's strange behavior during the last year or so of his life. As I also noted in my Introduction, von Neumann is the link between the Freud of the *Megalomania* manuscript and the contemporary cognitive sciences.

A FINAL NOTE

Fortunately, great thinkers pass away; we can write about them, judge them and ignore them. Many have left behind letters, manuscripts, notes, trinkets and other relics of lovers, ex-lovers and those they secretly pined after; they have hoped that future generations of scholars and philosophers would immerse themselves in their lives and thoughts; and they have thus sought to remain part of the contemporary scene, just as they had been an inseparable part of culture in their own day.

Freud—as is well-known—was not averse to such tactics. And yet the full range of his posthumous tricks went well beyond that of most great men. For at the end of his life, Freud decided to reinvent Freud.

He was lucky to have set these final thoughts on paper. He apparently believed that psychology would be far from becoming a true science more than half a century after he was gone. And it is certain that we are still very far from understanding the nature of logic, truth and lies. Even today there is no real science of the mind.

Scholars, psychologists and biographers can go on

from here, using Freud as the benchmark of their allegiance or superiority, revising his legacy and through their reinvention of Freud, revising some of the dominant ideas of the twentieth century.

Indeed, there can be little doubt that the publication of Freud's final essays has taken the wind out of the sails of those who had so prematurely dismissed him from center stage. For it was Freud's desire not to become but a footnote to history—his reluctance to fall from the Olympian heights he had known during his lifetime—that drove him to write his final masterpiece. I think we can all be grateful that he made this last heroic effort to cast a critical and uncompromising eye on the work of a lifetime. Perhaps he was right.[1]

---

[1] I cannot resist reporting a dream I had in Paris. *I was looking out of the hotel window toward the Eiffel Tower and an enormous lifelike image of a naked, fleshy Marilyn Monroe suddenly appeared atop the famous cast-iron structure. She hovered above the tower a few moments, then evaporated from sight, leaving a momentary view of the dark sky which was soon filled with an enormous image of Sigmund Freud blowing smoke rings and flicking cigar ashes over Paris. The sky erupted in fire and dark clouds. And as if from nowhere, Moses appeared, raised two enormous stone tablets above his head, swaying back and forth, and with a final, powerful movement of his arms thrust the tablets onto the city. Shattered pieces of stone bounced back into the sky. Moses, the bits of stone, the dark clouds and the fire gave way to Marilyn in* The Seven Year Itch, *holding her skirt as an unseen wind swept up under her. Followed by Freud once again, still blowing large rings of smoke but holding a manuscript high above his head, like the tablets that Moses had been smashing over the city. Then, as if aware of a presence, he looked straight at me and winked.* I awoke in a cold sweat.

I have no idea what any of that could mean.

ENDNOTES

Introduction

1. For example, Frederick Crews once wrote a famous Freudian analysis of Nathaniel Hawthorne, *The Sins of The Fathers: Hawthorne's Psychological Themes* (1966), in which he argued that Hawthorne's work was only interesting if read as a Freudian case study: "This, I think, is Hawthorne's distinction as a psychologist—not simply that his characters' seemingly freakish behavior can be matched by real-life examples, but that the total fabric of his plots manages to display fundamental yet elusive processes of the mind. Most importantly, those plots depict with incredible fidelity the results of unresolved Oedipal conflict" (p. 262). He then wrote a defense of psychoanalysis in *Out of My System: Psychoanalysis, Ideology and Critical Method* (1975), where he admitted to its limitations. Nonetheless, he continued to believe, "Psychoanalysis is the only psychology to have seriously altered our way of reading literature, and this alteration is little understood by the affected parties" (page 4). He came to see the error of his ways and, in the freer air of the post-Freudian period, has "decided to help others resist the fallacies to which I had succumbed in the 1960s," declaring, "I am *completely lacking in respect* for Freud" (F. Crews, *The Memory Wars*, 1995, italics in original, p. 293).

6. His 1928 paper, *"Zur Theorie der Gesellshaftsspiele," Math. Ann.* 100, 295–320, is often referred to as the seminal paper on Game Theory, the basis of mathematical models of games of chance such as poker and bridge. In his 1928 paper, von Neumann proved the "minimax theorem": there is always a rational course of action for two individuals in a competitive game

with completely opposed interests (player A wins means that player B must lose). In 1944 von Neumann and Oskar Morgenstern applied Game Theory to the study of economics. (See *Theory of Games and Economic Behavior,* Princeton, NJ: Princeton University Press, 1944.)

Game theory has had an enormous influence on the biological sciences. (See Endnote 14 below, and Norbert Weiner's comments in Endnote 5 to Anna Freud's paper on p. 170.)

But mathematicians and historians of science have noted that there are troubling questions of priority. In 1921 the French mathematician Émile Borel (1871–1956) first wrote about games of strategy and their applications to war and economics. (See Émile Borel, *La théorie du jeu et les équations intégrales à noyau symétrique gauche, Compte Rendu Acad. Sci. Paris,* vol. 173 (1921), pp. 1304–1308; also *Théories des Probabilités,* Paris, 1924; and *Compte Rendu Acad. Sci. Paris,* vol. 184 (1927), pp. 52–54. Von Neumann claimed he was not familiar with Borel's work and reportedly became very angry when he learned the papers had been translated into English in 1953. (See *Econometrica* 21 (1953), pp. 95–126, for Borel's papers and von Neumann's reply; and Steve J. Heims, *John von Neumann and Norbert Weiner: From Mathematics to the Technologies of Life and Death,* Cambridge, MA: MIT Press, 1980, pp. 83–84, and note 14, pp. 440–441.)

14. This list of major scientific theories—all part of the contemporary larger worldview—should, for the purposes of completeness, include, *Selfish Genes, Memes, Selection, Computations, Neural Networks, Game Theory* and the *Prisoner's Dilemma* and *Generative Grammars,* as well as the great scientific and mythical figures of our day: Mendel, Darwin, Turing, von Neumann, Weiner, Hamilton, Rosenblath and Chomsky. Furthermore, it is worth noting that one of the widely acclaimed "insights" of Game Theory came out of an international competition in which strategists were asked to decide on what pattern of "cooperation" and "defection" (noncooperation) would be most effective in many forms of competition. The winning strategy was *Tit for Tat*—cooperate at first and then do whatever your opponent did on his last move, defect if he defected, cooperate if he cooperated.

As the competition organizer wrote: "You do not have to do better than the other player to do well for yourself. . . . Letting each of them do the same or a little better than you is fine, as long as you tend to do well yourself. There is no point in being envious of the success of the other player, since in an iterated Prisoner's Dilemma of long duration the other's success is virtually a prerequisite of your doing well yourself" (Robert Axelrod, cited in Douglas R. Hofstadter, *Metamagical Themas: Questing for the Essence of Mind and Pattern*, New York: Basic Books, 1985, p. 727). I find this a rather curious claim, for with all their talk about blind genetic strategies ruthlessly determining human and animal behavior, contemporary scientists and philosophers seem guilt-ridden by the logic of their own arguments. They feel compelled to prove that nature wants us to cooperate as well. Tit for Tat is a perfect example of this need to find brotherly love among man and animals. Freud, in the *Manuscript*, makes no such compromises, and as a consequence, I believe his work is a far more penetrating study of human behavior. Indeed, it is the need to demonstrate "cooperation" in the human and animal worlds that leads to the rather absurd statement, already quoted, that *"there is no point in being envious of the success of the other player"*! And what, we might ask Professor Axelrod (the author of this piece of wisdom), is the point of being successful if everyone else is as well? The suggestion is as naive as the idea that it is possible to live in a world in which *everyone* is wealthy. Who would *serve* whom? The point of *being successful* is that we can boast about it, that we can say we're better than the others.

Chapter 2

1. Luc Tangorre, whose story is strikingly similar to that of Hans Hellbach described in the *Manuscript*, was first arrested in 1983 for a series of rapes committed between 1979 and 1981 in Marseilles. A committee for his defense included such notables as Françoise Sagan, Marguerite Duras, Claude Mauriac, Laurent Schwartz, Pierre Vidal-Naquet, etc. He was given a presidential pardon by the then French president, François Mitterand, in February 1988. In 1992 he was arrested and condemned for raping two young American women on the 23rd of May, 1988. (See

Pierre Vidal-Naquet's "Luc Tangorre et notre erreur," *Le Monde*, Samedi, 15 février 1992, pp. 1–2, where he admits to having been duped. See also *Le Monde*, 9–10 février, 1992, p. 9, for details of the trial.) The remarkable similarity to some aspects of the rape case described by Freud, as well as his discussion of the trial of Wagner-Jaurreg, lends considerable weight to his conclusions concerning certain fundamental aspects of the human psyche.

Chapter 8

1. I give here a sampling of some of the more adverse reactions to Freud's claim that authority is psychotic.

One scientist, who described his robot as "the most intelligent and knowledgeable machine built to date," wrote that "contrary to the view expressed in the *Manuscript* attributed to Sigmund Freud, the more intelligent the machine, the more rational it is. Freud has pandered to the commonplace view that great geniuses are mentally diseased. Science has now shown the opposite is the truth." Several philosophers scoffed at Freud's view of law in the second part of the paragraph. One political scientist wrote, "His failure to understand democracy comes from his deep-rooted need to project his own megalomania on society." Both a rabbi and a cardinal came to the defense of Moses and the Ten Commandments. "This is the work of the Devil," the cardinal wrote.

Finally, the following comments were from a historian of science: "Even if it had been done in a last-minute state of delirium (and it was too long and carefully thought out for that) the *Manuscript* is an inexcusable piece of trivia. Men of true stature never fall into deliriums. Freud is challenging the foundations of rational thought, the underpinnings of society and the psychological stability of his most ardent admirers and even his most fervent detractors.

"The *Manuscript* is a testimony not to Freud's greatness, but to the baseness of his character. What Freud was really all about was envy. And perhaps the best example of this on record is Freud's exchange of letters with Albert Einstein. Einstein had expressed doubts about Freud's work [See Jones, *op. cit.*, 3, 243]. Since Freud had little understanding of science and he could not have known what was yet to be discovered, in his small envious, petty way, he decided to leave behind a manuscript that would question the integrity of scientists in the years to come. The *Manuscript* proves the bankruptcy of Freudian thought."

Chapter 9

4. When Gulliver (like the hallucinatory superego) becomes gigantic compared to the Lilliputians—the Man Mountain—even the most trivial act on his part—brandishing his sword, shooting his pistol, sneezing, etc.—causes the poor Lilliputians to respond with awe, fear and admiration. Gulliver also plays with the enemy fleet like toys, much as Dicke plays with his Marilyn Machine. But the awe that he inspires is not associated with any morality. It's awe for awe's sake!

So too Alice seems to reflect the apparent "objectivity" of Freud's hallucinating superego when she asks, "Am I really myself?" Violence is an important part of Alice's world; animals are constantly being threatened with extinction in a world, again, without morals. And like the "sacred texts" of Freud's megalomaniac (Wagner's secret theory or Dicke's Loop Theory, etc.), Jabberwocky is also a sacred text, read in a moral vacuum. "The charm of Jabberwocky is that it is a code language," William Empson noted, "the language with which grown-ups hide things from children or children from grown-ups" (*Some Versions of the Pastoral*, New York: New Directions, 1960, p. 255).

Finally, let me note that Phyllis Greenacre captured some of Freud's hallucinatory superego when she wrote, "I came to the conclusion that fetishism, and perhaps other perversions of emotional development, occurred in people who were constitutionally active and strong, but subject at certain critical periods in early life to external stresses of a nature which upset the integrity of the self-perception and assimilation of the sensations of their own bodies. In other words, the body image becomes impaired; and the fetishistic perversion is an . . . attempt to stabilize this in such a way as to increase the capacity to utilize inherent aggressive and sexual drives. . . . One way in which this impairment . . . appeared was in disturbed subjective sensations of changing size of total body or of certain body parts" (*Swift and Carroll: A Psychoanalytic Study of Two Lives*, New York: International Universities Press, 1955, pp. 10–11). There may be an interesting relation between this view of emotions and that of Freud in the *Manuscript*, though Greenacre was always an orthodox Freudian and might not have wanted to associate herself with Freud's posthumous views.

Anna Freud:

Notes on a Conversation with Johnny von Neumann

5. Norbert Weiner, in his *Cybernetics: or Control and Communication in the Animal and Machine* (Cambridge, MA: MIT Press, 1948, 1960, p. 159) wrote the following about Game Theory:

> This theory is based on the assumption that each player, at every stage, in view of the information then available to him, plays in accordance with a completely intelligent policy, which will in the end assure of the greatest possible expectation of reward. . . . Even in the case of two players, the theory is complicated, although it often leads to the choice of a definite line of play. In many cases, however, where there are three players, and in the overwhelming majority of cases, when the number of players is large, the result is one of extreme indeterminacy and instability. The individual players are compelled by their own cupidity to form coalitions; but these coalitions do not generally establish themselves in any single, determinate way, and usually terminate in a welter of betrayal, turncoatism, and deception, as is only too true a picture of the higher business life, or the closely related lives of politics, diplomacy, and war. In the long run, even the most brilliant hucksters become tired of this and agree to live in peace with one another, and the great rewards are reserved for the one who watches for an opportune time to break his agreement and betray his companions.

CAST OF CHARACTERS

From the Imagined World

Professor Albert J. Stewart, annotator of the Freud *Manuscript*; colleague of Norman Dicke; coauthor with Dicke of numerous papers on Loop Theory.

Norman Dicke, Stewart's renowned colleague; Looker Laureate; creator of Loop Theory and the Marilyn Machine.

Debra, Dicke's former postdoc.

The Marilyn Machine, Dicke and colleagues' sexy creation.

Bernadette Schilder, a mysterious granddaughter of Sigmund Freud.

Emma Benesch-Schilder, Bernadette Schilder's mother; Freud's daughter by Adelaide Benesch.

Adelaide Benesch, Bernadette's grandmother (Emma's mother) whose affair with Freud had been, until the publication of these documents, a well-guarded secret.

Stefan Schilder, husband of Emma Benesch, father of Bernadette Schilder; killed by an automobile on Bernadette's first birthday.

Georg Probst, SS officer who had studied with Wagner and kept *Manuscript* that Adelaide Benesch had returned, unread, to Freud after the Anschluss.

Heinrich Probst, nephew of Georg Probst; inherits *Manuscript,* tries to publish it and eventually brings it to the Benesch-Schilder family in London after the war.

Hans Hellbach, an Austrian rapist, who won a presidential reprieve in the 1920s and was subsequently arrested for raping two women in southern Germany. Fought in World War I and was "successfully" treated by Wagner and Kozlowski for War Neurosis.

From the Reinvented World

Luc Tagorre, a French rapist who won a presidential reprieve more than half a century later. Stewart notes parallel to Hellbach case in Freud's *Manuscript.*

Julius Wagner-Jaurreg, Freud's lifelong friend from his days in medical school; Nobel Laureate (1928); his clinic treated soldiers considered "malingerers" with electric shock during First World War; Freud was "expert" witness at his "trial" in 1920.

Michael Kozlowski, Wagner's sadistic, lying colleague; not present at Wagner "trial" ; Wagner's obituary for Kozlowski in 1935 written only in Polish.

Gustave Eiffel, the constructor of the famous Eiffel Tower.

Maurice Koechlin, Eiffel's colleague; he and **Emile Nouguier** are the real inventors of the "Eiffel" Tower; tells Freud his story.

John von Neumann, major twentieth-century mathematician whose work was crucial to the development of the computer; creator of Game Theory (1928); visits Anna Freud in 1950s.

Émile Borel, important French mathematician, wrote first known papers on Game Theory (1921); von Neumann challenged their importance (1953).

Norbert Weiner, creator of cybernetics; critical of Game Theory.

Anna Freud, Freud's daughter; comes upon Freud writing *Manuscript,* but never asks him what he is writing; dies before *Manuscript* is discovered; meets with von Neumann.

Sigmund Freud, writes at length about the failings of his own work and presents us with a startling new view of the problems of the mind.

Moses, an obsession of Freud's; presumed author of the Ten Commandments; one of the first documented cases of megalomania.